A Cur

Olga, the fortune-teller, clutched the table edge. "Listen to me," she said to Piper. "You are in grave danger. The circus is not safe for you. Keep away."

Piper shook her head. "You have the wrong Halliwell," she said, trying to laugh off the warning. "My sister Prue is the one with the circus hang-up."

Olga sank down into her chair. "All around you, I can sense an unusual energy field. It attracts darkness," she said.

Okay, I'm officially freaked out now, Piper thought. She wondered if Olga had what the Gypsies called "the gift of second sight." Maybe the woman's act wasn't bogus after all.

"There are evil forces at work at the Carnival Cavalcade," Olga said. "You see only pretty lights, hear the happy music. That is a mask to cover up the dark forces at work here. You must take great care."

"But how am I in danger?" Piper asked.

Olga shut her eyes. Her breath came in choking gasps. She let out a low moan. "A curse is afoot," she muttered. "It moves toward you." Olga's eyes popped open again. "That is all I can say. You must leave."

Charmed™

Published by Simon & Schuster

THE GYPSY ENCHANTMENT

An original novel by Carla Jablonski

Based on the hit TV series created by

Constance M. Burge

SIMON PULSE

New York London Toronto Sydney Singapore

This book is a work of fiction. Any references to historical events, real people, or real locales are used fictitiously. Other names, characters, places, and incidents are the product of the author's imagination and any resemblance to actual events or locales or persons, living or dead, is entirely coincidental.

First Simon Pulse edition September 2002
™ & © 2001 Spelling Television Inc. All Rights Reserved.

 SIMON PULSE
An imprint of Simon & Schuster
Children's Publishing Division
1230 Avenue of the Americas
New York, NY 10020

First Pocket Pulse printing February 2001

Printed in the United States of America

10 9 8 7 6 5

ISBN 0-7434-1235-4

THE GYPSY ENCHANTMENT

CHAPTER
1

Prue felt the presence behind her. Was that one creature or two? She studied the two-headed shadow on the floor in front of her. She could tell from the shadow's outline that the thing behind her was humanlike, but the body looked like a big blob. Each head was oddly shaped, and in profile she could make out their strange noses.

"Just what I don't need," she muttered. "I'm late as it is." Standing awkwardly on one high heel, she whirled around and hurled the strappy sandal in her hand at the interloper.

"Hey!" Phoebe shouted as Piper shrieked and ducked. "Watch it."

Prue smirked at her sisters. "You thought you could sneak up and scare me? After all the demon training I've had? You're bigger clowns than I thought."

Prue's eyes traveled up and down her sisters' outlandish costumes. They wore oversize overalls stuffed with pillows. Piper had tucked her long dark hair under a bright orange wig made of yarn. Phoebe wore a crushed fedora so big that it slipped down to her eyebrows. Both had little red balls stuck on their noses.

"The answer is still no," Prue declared. "No matter how easily you would fit in."

"No fair," Phoebe complained. "We're the ones who love the circus, and you're the one with the cush assignment."

"There is nothing 'cush' about this job," Prue grumbled. The magazine she often worked for as a freelance photojournalist, *415*, had paired Prue with a reporter doing a feature story on the Carnival Cavalcade—a carnival with circus acts that performed in a tent set up in Golden Gate Park. They were going to spend the whole week "amidst the sawdust and spangles," as Kristin McMillan, the reporter Prue would be working with, had so colorfully put it.

"I wish this week was over already," Prue said with a sigh.

"Your whole attitude makes it even more of a shame," Piper protested. "We should go—not you. You hate the circus."

Prue eyed her sisters again. "Especially clowns."

"Okay, so maybe the clown getup wasn't the best way to persuade you to take us with you," Piper admitted. "But you have to admit, it got your attention."

"And nearly got you beaned by my sandal." Prue retrieved her shoe and stepped into it.

"But we deserve to go," Phoebe whined.

Prue shook her head as she bent over to buckle the strap of her sandal. "You sound like a six-year-old." She straightened up and put her hands on her hips. "Well, you certainly look as if you belong at the circus."

Prue bit her lip as her sisters put on their most pleading, pathetic expressions. She fought back a laugh. "Okay, you can come. But hurry," she added sternly. "I'm already running behind."

"Whoo-hoo!" Phoebe cheered. She and Piper slapped high fives, then dashed out of Prue's bedroom.

I hope I don't regret this, Prue thought. This is a professional situation, and those two are acting like out-of-control toddlers. I'll have enough to worry about as it is.

Prue knew that her sisters imagined being assigned to cover the carnival was just fun and games, but she knew it was going to be a tough gig. She would be trying to capture the essence of live performance, snap backstage antics, and also do intimate individual portraits. Different techniques, approaches, film, and lenses would be called for in each situation. That meant a lot of switching gears and staying alert to potential images and visual moments, in addition to keeping track of f-stops and light readings.

But there was a deeper reason Prue was on edge about this assignment.

She knew she was being silly, but her sisters were right: Prue just didn't like the circus. There wasn't anything she could quite put her finger on that explained her aversion. Circuses and carnivals simply gave her the creeps and always had. The transient lifestyle cloaked the performers and staff in anonymity, creating an air of mystery that Prue found unsettling.

After all, Prue continued musing as she ran a brush through her thick dark hair, who knows *who* is under all that clown makeup? What normal person would think it was fun to step into cages with tigers, or balance three chairs on her chin?

She scanned her bedroom to make sure she hadn't forgotten anything. Camera case loaded with both black-and-white and color film, flashes, and batteries. Purse with comb, lipstick, mints, and cell phone. All she needed now was to find her keys, corral her sisters, and head out.

"Ready!" Phoebe posed in the doorway in a pair of black jeans and a blue halter top. "You see? Goodbye clown, hello hottie."

"I don't know if there will be anyone there to appreciate your finer qualities," Prue commented. "Who are you trying to impress, the elephants?"

"Are you kidding?" Phoebe's dark eyes widened. "The circus is full of hunky riggers and roustabouts. Guys with serious muscle power. Besides, you're the one with the clown problem, not me."

"I'd really hate to think the circus is your new dating pool," Prue said.

Phoebe laughed. "Most of the guys I meet are clowns anyway. At least this way they have an excuse."

Piper came to join them. Her bright red-and-white sundress looked perfect for a day at the carnival. "Leave it to Phoebe to see a day at the circus as a way to cruise guys."

"Speaking of leaving," Prue said. "First stop, Muffin Madness. I need to pick up some breakfast since I don't know when I'll have a chance to grab something once we're there."

She hustled her sisters out the door and to the car. She slid behind the wheel with Piper beside her. Phoebe sprawled across the backseat. Prue drove the familiar route to the muffin shop.

"So what exactly is this assignment?" Phoebe asked after they divvied up their bags of coffee and muffins. "I'm glad you have this job so that we get to go, but don't circuses usually have their own publicity machine?"

"She's right," Piper added. "Why would they bring in an outside photographer?"

Prue kept her eye on the traffic as she headed toward Golden Gate Park. "This is a backstage story. You know, the behind-the-scenes stuff that isn't in the typical press kit."

Piper flicked her sunglasses up onto her head and looked at Prue. "Behind the scenes? Does that mean what I think it means?"

Prue could hear the excitement in her sister's voice.

Phoebe leaned in between her sisters. "You'll have an all-access pass? Cool!"

"I don't know if that means that *you'll* have access," Prue warned. "This is actually quite unusual. Kristin explained that the only reason the owner, Mr. Amalfi, is allowing us backstage is because he's hoping the article will help ticket sales. I think they've been somewhat lower than he'd hoped."

"Why is going backstage unusual?" Piper asked.

"Circuses tend to be pretty closed communities," Prue explained. "Kristin told me to be prepared for some less-than-willing participants."

"Kristin," Phoebe repeated. "Have we met her?"

"Kristin McMillan," Prue said. "Short blond hair, seriously perky."

"Oh, yeah," Phoebe murmured. "The cheerleader type."

Prue grinned. "That's her. Only I think she would outpep the pep squad."

"You can't stand her," Piper observed.

"That's not true," Prue protested. "Well, not exactly true. Not completely." She sighed. "Okay, I find her style sort of clashes with mine."

"You see? You need us," Piper said. "Otherwise you might strangle the perky right out of her."

Prue laughed. "You're probably right." She turned into the park. "Okay, I'm glad you're here. If only to balance out Kristin's niceness."

"Are you insulting us?" Piper asked. "Implying that we, your lovely sisters, aren't nice?"

Prue grinned and went on as if she hadn't heard Piper's protest. "You know, yin yang, balance of energies. Kristin is overly nice and you two are—"

"We get it, we get it," Piper grumbled. "Still, it's nice to be needed." She patted Prue's shoulder and then giggled.

We do need each other, Prue thought, grinning at Piper. We're so different but so alike.

Ever since the Halliwell sisters came into their powers, their ties to one another had become even stronger. In fact, if they hadn't discovered that they were witches, they might never have worked so hard to overcome those differences. Nothing like fending off warlocks to bring a family together, Prue mused. She was glad her sisters had insisted on tagging along today. But she wasn't going to let them know that. She'd never live it down!

Prue checked the directions Kristin had given her to the "backstage" entrance. Actually, it was a security check-in point near the trailers that housed the performers. Several men carrying clipboards and walkie-talkies stood chatting just inside the police barricades that ran completely around the area. Prue pulled into the parking lot and stopped the car.

Almost instantly, Phoebe and Piper scrambled out. "Hey, wait for me," Prue called after them.

No use. Piper and Phoebe were so excited that they hurried up to the sawhorse barricades and ducked under them. A burly guard instantly headed their way. Those two really are behaving like six-year-olds, Prue observed.

Prue shook her head with amusement as she pulled out her equipment. She regretted her choice of shoes almost instantly. The ground was slightly soggy from recent rains, and she realized that inside the tent there would be dirt and sawdust. Expensive high-heel sandals were not the smartest choice, she was thinking as she caught up to her sisters.

The guard was eyeing Piper and Phoebe suspiciously. "I don't see your names here," he said, scanning his clipboard. "If you're not on the list, you need to go to the front and buy tickets like everyone else."

"Prue Halliwell," Prue announced to the security guard.

He glanced down at his clipboard. "You check out. Kristin McMillan asked me to have you meet her at the cookhouse trailer up ahead and to the left. She was having breakfast with some of the performers."

"Thanks." Prue tried to think of a way to get Piper and Phoebe passes. Maybe she could ask Kristin to arrange the passes for them.

Phoebe wasted no time in coming up with a scheme. "We're Ms. Halliwell's assistants." Phoebe grabbed the camera accessories case out of Prue's grip and the brown paper bag holding her coffee and half-nibbled muffin. Phoebe handed the bag to Piper, who nodded.

The guard didn't seem to be buying it. He raised a skeptical eyebrow. Phoebe got closer to him and jerked her head in Prue's direction. "She's a real prima donna," Phoebe told the guard in a throaty stage whisper. "Afraid she'll break a nail. You know the type."

Piper nodded and rolled her eyes in Prue's direction. "Makes us carry everything," she confided.

"But the good news is," Phoebe went on, "Miss Thing's brattiness keeps us employed."

Prue fought back a grin. She decided to play along. "Why are you chatting when there is work to do?" she snapped. "And someone please wipe off my shoes before they are ruined." Might as well get the most mileage out of this, she thought.

"Shoes?" Prue repeated, adding an incredulous edge to her voice. She glared at Piper, then at Phoebe, as if cleaning her shoes was the most important task in the world.

Piper gave Prue a dark look, then bent down and wiped the shoes with a napkin from the brown paper bag. Prue had a feeling she'd pay for this little charade, but hey—if they wanted her to play prima donna she had to be convincing, right?

"Okay, here are the passes." The security guard gave them their credentials—tags hanging from cords to wear around their necks. Prue saw that each had "All access" printed on it, along with the date. He waved them through, then rejoined the other security guards. Prue felt their eyes on her and her sisters as they passed the group.

"Phoebe, yesterday's lunch was not acceptable," Prue continued for the guard's benefit. "I've told you a thousand times, the dressing must be on the side, and the salad absolutely crisp or it is inedible."

Once they moved out of the guard's earshot, Prue dropped the diva routine. "I can't believe you called me a brat," she chided her sisters.

"Ooh, she's being a brat again," Piper teased.

"Ha ha." Prue scanned the area. This part of Golden Gate Park had been transformed into a mini trailer city. Beyond the trailers was the midway, set up along the wide boulevards that graced the center of the park. In the distance she could see the top of the circus tent, where the performances would take place several times a day and into the evening. She knew there were more trailers set up on the other side of the tent.

"Okay," Prue said. "He told us to find Kristin near the cookhouse trailer. But which one is that?"

"Oh, Prue," a singsong voice called. Prue turned toward the familiar tone. Kristin McMillan stood in front of a trailer that had many people—some in costumes, some in street clothes—swarming around it.

"Must be food," Piper said. "Look at the crowd."

Kristin waved at them. "Over here." Prue thought that Kristin's trademark pink suit made her look even more like the former cheerleader she'd been. Prue had always wondered how Kristin managed to find so many outfits in that single shade of pink. Didn't she ever want to rebel and wear blue? Or even—gasp!—black?

Kristin flashed Prue a perfect smile, and then went back to talking to the three clowns surrounding her.

"Oh, goody. The fun begins now," Prue grumbled.

"You are so weird," Piper commented. "You can kick demon booty but you can't handle clowns?"

"I'll take a demon or a warlock over a clown any day," Prue replied. And I'm only half kidding, she added to herself.

Phoebe gave her a mock shocked expression. "Take that back this instant," she scolded. "We Halliwells have a tendency to get what we wish for."

Prue sighed. Phoebe was right. Calling up demons even in jest tended to bring rather dangerous results.

CHAPTER 2

"Prue, great! Perfect timing!" Kristin smiled broadly as Prue headed across the gravel toward the group. Phoebe and Piper followed a few steps behind her.

Why is it that everything Kristin says sounds as if she's about to burst into a cheer? Prue wondered. Does the woman ever speak without an exclamation point at the end of every sentence?

Kristin stood with three clowns. One of them was very tall, the other nearly as round as she was high. The third had such elaborate makeup that at first glance Prue thought he was wearing a mask. Once she got closer, though, she could see he had applied a putty nose, extended his chin, and applied thick gobs of gold goop to his skin. The effect was quite striking. Prue was surprised to find herself thinking he looked very regal. Instead of typical clown baggy pants, he wore a tuxedo. Then she realized the jacket was made of stretchy material—sort of leotard formal

11

wear. The close-fitting costume certainly emphasized his buff body, Prue observed. Her eyes traveled up from his shapely legs to his face. The makeup reminded Prue of a fanciful illustration of the man in the moon. When he turned sideways, his profile—with his jutting chin and curved nose—resembled a crescent moon.

She was startled when he made a bouquet of flowers appear out of nowhere and handed it to her.

"Uh, thanks," Prue said, wondering what she should do with the paper bouquet. She didn't have to think long. The girl clown snatched the flowers away and began beating the Man-in-the-Moon clown with them. The tall clown stepped in between them as they went into a mock fight. Then the girl came at Prue.

I hate audience participation, Prue thought, gritting her teeth. The girl waggled her fingers in front of Prue's face as if she was scolding her, honking a hidden horn the whole time.

Oo-kay, I'm ready for this little performance to be over now. Prue kept a small smile plastered on her face so that no one would realize how annoyed she actually was.

Kristin was laughing hysterically, bending over double and gasping for breath. Phoebe and Piper were egging on the clowns.

"You have to watch out for her," Piper told the girl clown. "She'll try to steal your boyfriend every time."

"Piper!" Prue scolded.

Meanwhile, Phoebe was insisting the Man-in-the-Moon clown continue pursuing Prue. "I can tell she loves you," Phoebe declared theatrically. The clown flung himself to his knees in front of Prue, seeming to beg for her hand.

The girl clown leaped on him and climbed onto his shoulders, smacking his head furiously. He acted as if he didn't know where she was, completely baffled by the blows to his head. Finally, the tall clown plucked the girl from the Man-in-the-Moon clown's back and seated her atop his own shoulders, where she was safely out of reach.

Prue applauded, hoping that would signal it was now time to end the act. It seemed to work. Phoebe, Piper, and Kristin joined in; Phoebe even put two fingers into her mouth and let out a shrieking whistle. As a finale, the girl clown leaped off the tall clown's shoulders into the waiting arms of the Man-in-the-Moon clown.

"Oh, that was so great!" Kristin gushed. "Wasn't that great?"

"Great," Prue muttered.

As the handsome clown lowered the girl clown to the ground, the tall clown bent down to shake Prue's hand. "I'm Kaboodle," he said. "This is my wife, Masha."

The round clown bowed. "And this is Sacha," she said, with a gesture to the handsome clown, who nodded.

"We're going to be featuring Kaboodle and Masha," Kristin explained. "They've been with the Carnival Cavalcade the longest of any of the performers, and they do something really wonderful. Tell about the Caring Clown Company."

"Happily," Kaboodle said. Prue was pretty sure he

said that with a grin, but since a gigantic red smile dominated his painted face, it was hard to tell, even this close.

"Masha and I started the project several years ago," Kaboodle said. "We wanted to do something for kids, beyond just performing in the shows. So we round up volunteers each season to join us at children's wards in hospitals in each of the towns we visit."

"The kids really do seem to appreciate it," Masha added. "But I think we love it even more than they do."

"We're trying to get Sacha to join in, but so far he's been somewhat reluctant," Kaboodle said.

"Don't give him a hard time," Masha scolded her husband. "First of Mays have enough to worry about without adding extra duties to their schedules."

Prue's brow wrinkled. "First of Mays?" she repeated.

Masha let out a bellowing laugh. "Sorry, dearie. Insider speak. A First of May is a new clown. Sacha just joined us this season."

Does Sacha speak? Prue wondered. As if in answer, Masha added, "Don't mind him. He's the strong, silent type. Each of us has a unique persona. I'm round, Kaboodle is tall, and Sacha is—"

"Silent?" Prue finished for her.

Sacha grinned and bowed.

"You'll find a lot of the performers won't drop their personas around you, since you're outsiders," Kaboodle said.

"Some of them don't even drop them around us," Masha added. She leaned into Prue. Prue could smell the greasepaint and powder. "I have heard him speak, however. But I've actually never seen him without makeup. All the girls on the show are wondering if he's as handsome as we suspect. Isn't that right, Sacha?"

Sacha rolled his eyes in an exaggerated fashion, then strutted around as if he were a parading peacock. Piper and Phoebe pretended to swoon.

Kaboodle laughed. "You two are naturals," he told them.

"I'll second that," Prue said.

"You know, we're looking for local volunteers to continue visiting the children after we leave. Would you be interested?" Masha asked Piper and Phoebe.

"That sounds fantastic," Piper said.

Phoebe grinned at Prue. "We'll become your worst nightmare," she teased her older sister. "A pair of clowns living under your roof."

"You're already borderline buffoons," Prue teased back.

Phoebe made a face at Prue, then asked Kaboodle more questions on how to volunteer.

"Let's get some shots of these three," Kristin said. "We have several interviews scheduled."

Sacha, Masha, and Kaboodle went into various poses as Prue snapped pictures. The day was sunny and bright, so she didn't need to set up lights or flashes.

"Okay," Kristin said, consulting her notepad. "Let's go over my list. Obviously, we'll want some action shots in the ring."

"I brought all different speeds of film," Prue assured her. "I figured I would do those shots in color and the interviews in black and white."

"Great." Kristin flashed a high wattage grin. "That will give us lots of moods. Today we'll be talking to Mr. Amalfi, the owner and ringmaster, and Ivan the Gypsy Violinist."

Sacha dropped the top hat he was balancing. "Ivan?" he said.

Everyone's heads whipped toward Sacha. He had been silent up until now. That one word had an impact.

"Is something wrong?" Masha asked.

"Perhaps you should interview the Flying Cantonellis," Sacha suggested, retrieving his hat. "They do a wonderful aerial act. I believe that would be better than interviewing Ivan."

Prue detected an accent but couldn't place it. She also was aware that Sacha seemed worried or concerned about their making contact with Ivan.

"Why shouldn't we talk to this Ivan?" she asked. Could Sacha be jealous of the performer? Did he want to keep the spotlight on his own act?

"Ivan's act is very special," Kristin said. "He's being featured. My editor was quite specific. So was Mr. Amalfi, the circus owner."

"Forgive me." Sacha gave a small bow. "I spoke out of turn. I don't like to speak ill of performers behind their backs. Let me just say that Ivan is not a problem. However, trouble seems to find him. Take care."

Sort of like us charmed Halliwells, Prue thought. Trouble tends to find us, too.

She noticed Kaboodle and Masha exchange a serious glance. "Is Sacha right?" she asked them. "Should we avoid Ivan?"

Kaboodle looked uncomfortable. "There are people here who feel that Ivan has bad luck this season. Things have occurred . . ."

"Some believe Ivan is cursed," Sacha insisted.

"Now, Sacha," Masha said, a warning tone in her voice.

"I'm only saying what is widely known," Sacha protested.

"What a great angle!" Kristin exclaimed. "The cursed Gypsy. Circus superstitions! Fantastic!"

There are those exclamation points again, Prue thought.

Kristin checked her watch. "Ivan is waiting for us in his trailer right now. Let's go."

Prue took a picture of her two sisters horsing around with the clowns. "Aha! Now I have incriminating evidence to use against you," she teased. Then she gathered up her belongings.

"Enjoy the show!" Kaboodle cried. Then the three clowns tumbled away. Literally.

Prue shook her head watching them. How do they do that? They must be made of rubber springs.

"That wasn't so bad, was it, sis?" Piper asked Prue.

"I lived," Prue replied.

"I think they are so cute!" Phoebe said. "I definitely want to check out volunteering." Prue watched her sister's gaze wander to some seriously buff circus employees. "Only right now, I think I'd like to check out the action on the midway."

"Do you have your passes?" Prue asked.

"Got 'em," Piper said. Phoebe nodded.

"See you after the show. Just wait in the tent so we can find each other."

"Deal."

"Come on, Prue," Kristin called. She was walking briskly away from the trailers. "We don't want to keep Ivan waiting."

"Coming." Prue waved good-bye to her sisters, then turned to follow Kristin.

Ewwwww! What is that disgusting, squishy feeling between my toes. Prue glanced down. Oh, gross! That looks like . . . Yes. Elephant poop!

"Great," Prue muttered. "This Ivan person's bad luck is already rubbing off on me. What next?"

CHAPTER
3

Piper took in a deep breath. Her nose crinkled. She could smell the sweet scent of cotton candy mixed with popcorn, sweat, and animals. It was a very earthy smell, and she liked it. She enjoyed feeling the warmth of the sun on her bare arms and the bustling crowd around her.

She just didn't get Prue's attitude toward the circus. What's not to like? She felt ten years old again. A welcome feeling, given all the demon busting she and her sisters had been involved in. It felt great to escape from the serious business of protecting innocents and protecting themselves from warlocks bent on killing them.

The lilting, hooting music of a calliope made her break into a broad smile. It was such a silly sound, filled with goofy exuberance.

She glanced at Phoebe. Her sister was obviously as caught up in the carefree sense of freedom. Phoebe was bending over to watch a clown paint a child's face. The little girl giggled with delight and Phoebe giggled along with her.

"Hey, pretty lady, would you like a hat?" Piper glanced over at a booth where a cute young man with shaggy blond hair was twisting balloons into all kinds of impossible shapes. He held out a swan to Piper.

"I'm supposed to wear that?" she asked, laughing.

The guy carefully fitted the swan atop Piper's head. "Beautiful." He winked. "And the hat's not bad either."

Piper fished around in her bag and gave the guy a dollar. He didn't even look old enough to have graduated from college yet.

"Ooh, what'd you get?" Phoebe darted up beside Piper. She smirked when she saw the balloon swan sitting on Piper's head. "Gee, Piper. It's so you."

"Another gorgeous girl. I'll have to come up with something extra special for you." The guy twisted the balloon and suddenly Phoebe had a pink giraffe sitting on her head.

"You see?" Piper said. "Don't fight it. He's irresistible."

"You're right. I have to have this." Phoebe reached into her jeans pocket and pulled out a bill. She dropped it into the guy's tip jar.

"I'd rather have your phone numbers," the guy said.

"Sorry," Piper said with a smile. "We only go out with grown-ups."

She slipped her arm through Phoebe's, and they hurried away giggling.

They passed a mother trying to console a small crying child. The ice cream on the pavement in front of the little girl told Piper the whole story. She reached up and removed her swan balloon hat and handed it to the little girl. The tears instantly stopped.

"Thank you," the mother said warmly.

"Thank you," the little girl said, never taking her eyes off the balloon hat.

Piper grinned. Some problems are a cinch to solve. She and Phoebe continued along the midway.

Phoebe scanned the crowd. "This place is full of some serious stud muffins," she commented.

"Want to try your luck?" a handsome booth operator called. Large muscles bulged under his red T-shirt. He held out three rings.

"Sure," Phoebe said.

The man eyed Phoebe's giraffe hat. Piper covered her mouth to hide her grin. Phoebe had obviously forgotten about the balloon hat and was concentrating on heavy flirting with Game Boy.

"So how is this game played?" Phoebe asked. She leaned onto the counter, gazing up at the hunk from under her thick eyelashes.

"It would probably be easier without the wildlife," the guy said.

"Huh?"

Piper tugged on Phoebe's sleeve and pointed at her head. Phoebe's hands flew up to the balloon critter. "Oh, right."

She removed the hat and smoothed her hair. "Let's try this again," she said. "So how does this game work?"

"Ooh, girlie, don't lose your money to that scam artist," a gruff voice said. "Jim, I see you're up to your old tricks."

Piper turned to check out who had given them the warning. Yikes! A burly man sporting multiple tattoos stood behind them. The buzz cut, the three earrings, the tattered black shirt, and the tattoos weren't what made Piper gasp out loud. It was the enormous snake draped over the man's shoulders!

"Give me a break, Ralphie," Jim, the booth operator, complained. "These girls might actually believe you."

Ralphie took a step toward Piper and Phoebe. Piper shrank up against the booth's wall. She had to force herself not to use her magical power to freeze the dude in his tracks. She really didn't want that snake to come any closer.

"Watch out for this one," Ralphie said, waggling a finger at the booth guy. "And it's Raphael, thank you very much." He made a little bow to Phoebe. "And whom do I have the pleasure of addressing?"

Phoebe's eyes widened as she stared at the snake. The snake stared back.

"Any time a pretty customer arrives, Ralphie-boy tries to horn in," Jim complained. But Piper could tell he was actually quite fond of Ralphie. She wondered how he felt about the snake—eew—which was flicking its tongue right at her.

"Oh, don't let Isabella scare you, missy," Raphael said. "She just wants to get to know you better. Don't you, sweetums." Double ewww. He just gave the snake a kiss on the lips. If snakes have lips.

Raphael stepped closer to Phoebe. He was practically drooling. Piper was relieved to see that the snake wasn't.

Phoebe seemed more disturbed by Raphael than the snake. "Sh-she is kind of pretty," Phoebe said uncertainly.

"Go ahead, sweetie. Pet her." Raphael held the snake out. It curled and then stretched toward Phoebe. Piper was stunned to see Phoebe stroke the snake's head.

Raphael grinned as the snake wriggled up Phoebe's arm. Piper's stomach flip-flopped watching the creature slither onto Phoebe's shoulder.

"Now your turn," Raphael said. He faced Piper. He held the snake's other end and made a move as if he was about to drape the thing across her shoulders.

"Uh, no, I don't think . . ." Piper backed up.

Luckily, she heard someone behind her call her name.

"Gotta go! Someone's calling!" Piper whirled around, leaving Phoebe with Raphael and the snake. Well, Phoebe's a big girl, Piper figured. She can take care of herself, and she didn't seem all that bothered by Isabella.

"Piper, over here!" the voice called again. Piper had already darted a few yards away from Raphael and the snake before she even glanced around to see who had called her name.

She was startled when she did. A tall twelve-year-old girl raced toward Piper, shouting her name the whole way.

"Jenny?" Piper said.

Behind Jenny was a tall, handsome guy. Piper's heart beat a little faster seeing his strong jaw, high cheekbones, and dark gray eyes. "And Dan. Of course," Piper said.

When Piper had stopped dating Dan it was one of the hardest things she had ever had to do. Harder than vanquishing evil. At least when you're fighting demons, she thought, you have no doubts that you're doing the right thing. And you're not hurting someone you care about. It's a black-and-white issue. But with Dan . . .

Piper shook her head. You did the right thing, she told herself. Your feelings for Leo are just too strong, and you had to give that relationship a fair chance.

Still, the echoes of her feelings for Dan welled up in her, mirrored in the wistful look that appeared in his eyes. That look vanished, replaced by a guarded wariness.

He obviously wasn't sure how she'd react to seeing him.

Jenny, however, was thrilled. Her broad grin said it all.

Dan's niece, Jenny, was the reason the Halliwells had met their handsome next-door neighbor Dan. She had been visiting him when she needed some girl-input. Piper stepped in to help—and into Dan's life. Only later she found she needed to step back out.

Piper sighed. Why isn't anything ever easy? she thought for what seemed to be the millionth time.

Jenny flung her arms around Piper. "Piper! This is so great! I'm so glad to see you."

Piper stumbled a few steps backward, caught off balance by Jenny's fervent bear hug, but also from seeing Dan.

"Hi," Dan said. She could hear the caution in his voice.

Piper tucked a strand of hair behind her ear. "Hi," she replied.

Jenny was beaming. "I can't believe we ran into you. Now maybe this stupid circus won't be so boring."

"Boring?" Piper repeated. She was surprised by Jenny's attitude.

Jenny rolled her eyes. "Uncle Dan just thinks I'm a total baby. This is for little kids."

"I don't know," Piper said. "I'm having a great time."

Looking at Jenny, she remembered how she had felt when she was Jenny's age. She had wanted to be grown-up so badly that anything that smacked of childishness was a total turnoff.

"What are you doing here?" Jenny asked.

"Prue has a photography assignment here. So she finagled us some passes."

"Do you get to go backstage and everything?" Jenny asked, new interest lighting her bright brown eyes.

Piper nodded. She was highly aware of Dan's silence. She was also aware that she hadn't looked directly at him since first seeing him. Is it always going to be this awkward? she asked herself.

Jenny turned to Dan and grabbed his arm. "Let's hang out with Piper!" she begged. She tugged his arm as she pleaded. Dan's eyes flicked to Piper's.

"Well, I suspect those passes won't cover everybody," Dan said.

Piper knew he was tactfully trying to let her off

the hook, but she couldn't help feeling a twinge seeing Jenny's disappointed face.

"Well, we might be able to work things out," Piper said slowly.

"It would probably be easier to swing if it's just the girls," Dan offered.

Piper was grateful that he had found a comfortable way to bow out.

"It will be more fun to hang with Piper than me anyway, right?" he added to Jenny.

"Totally," Jenny announced.

Dan laughed at how enthusiastically she agreed with him. "Hmm. I think I've just been insulted."

"It's a girl thing," Piper said.

"Right." Jenny beamed.

"So, we'll just drop Jenny off later this evening," Piper told Dan. "We're staying for the late show, too."

Dan nodded. "Sounds like a plan." He turned to Jenny. "Try not to be a brat."

"Dan—" Jenny protested.

Dan stuck his tongue out at her. She rolled her eyes. "You're the brat," she retorted.

"Have fun." Dan gave Piper one last wistful look and then vanished into the crowd.

Piper felt another pang as she watched him go. Snap out of it, she ordered herself. He's doing just fine without you, and you are happy with Leo. Dan is the past. Keep him there.

Jenny let out a loud theatrical sigh. "I wish you and Dan never broke up."

Oh, great. Here we go. Buckle up for the guilt trip. How to handle this? Where did Phoebe run off to? She'd provide a welcome distraction.

"I know you do, sweetie," Piper told Jenny. "But sometimes things just aren't meant to be."

"But you were perfect together. And he was much happier before," Jenny said firmly. "I know that for sure."

This time it was Piper who sighed. She really wanted off this topic. "Oh, look at that cotton candy machine. I could go for some, couldn't you?"

Without waiting for an answer, Piper lightly pushed Jenny toward the cotton candy maker. "We'll have two of your biggest and fluffiest," she told the vendor. And extra sticky to occupy Jenny's mouth, she added silently.

They took the paper cones and fed on the sugary airy substance. Wandering along the crowded midway, Piper wondered if all of San Francisco had turned out today. Piper steered Jenny around some strollers and dropped her sticky paper cone into a trash can.

"Yum," Piper said, licking her fingers. Jenny gobbled the last airy bit of pink fluff, then tossed her paper cone into the trash, too.

"Want to try some games?" Piper suggested. "Maybe we can win some stuffed animals."

Jenny's brow crinkled as she scanned the midway and all its milling crowds. "I don't know what to do first," she admitted. "Can we just try everything?"

Piper smiled. "Sure!" She would have said the exact same thing when she was Jenny's age. "Phoebe and I promised to meet Prue in the tent after the first show to regroup," she told Jenny. She glanced at her watch. "Which is fairly soon."

Piper blew a stray hair out of her face. She didn't

want to touch it with her still-sticky fingers. "Tell you what. Let's find a place to wash up, then we'll pick one thing to do before the show. Then, afterward, we'll come up with a new game plan. Phoebe may want to join us."

"Sounds good to me," Jenny agreed happily.

When Piper discovered that the nearest facilities were only the portable toilets, she bought some bottled water. She and Jenny used it to wash off their cotton-candy hands.

"Clean enough," Piper declared. "Now what?"

In their unsuccessful search for a rest room, Piper and Jenny had wound up on the outskirts of the midway. The booths were spaced farther apart here, and the trees clustered closer together.

"What's that?" Jenny asked.

Piper glanced where Jenny was pointing. A colorful wagon was tucked between two huge trees. A striped canvas awning shaded a rickety card table. Two chairs sat on either side of the table.

"I don't know," Piper said. "Why don't we check it out?"

Piper and Jenny strolled over to the wagon. As Piper got closer she could see how ornately decorated it was. Every inch of it was carved and painted. Gold leaf had been applied to what Piper realized were characters representing the zodiac. Moons, planets, and stars were embossed in silver. Stylized floral designs ran along the top and bottom of the wooden sides, and red and green swirls filled all the space in between. A chimney poked up toward the front of the wagon, where there was a seat for a driver. Piper wondered where the horses were, as it was obviously meant to travel using real *horse* horse-power.

"It's beautiful," Jenny murmured.

"It certainly is," Piper agreed.

A tall, slim woman in purple leggings and an oversize white sweater stepped out of the wagon. She was followed by a heavy-set older woman dressed in an elaborate Gypsy costume. Gold coins dangled from the edges of a scarf that was wrapped around her head. She wore several layers of petticoats and a bright red overskirt. Her vest was richly embroidered, and another embroidered scarf was tied around her thick waist. Her white blouse had soft, draping sleeves, which were rolled up to reveal multiple bracelets on each sturdy arm.

The young woman smoothed back her auburn hair. She tapped a small velvet bag that dangled from a cord around her neck.

Piper started. That looks like a charm bag, she thought.

"Thank you so much, Olga," the auburn-haired woman said.

"I must warn you, Miranda," Olga said in a raspy, heavily accented voice. "You have your sights on the wrong man. And there is nothing in that charm that can protect you from the grief he will bring."

The woman tossed her head. "You're wrong," she insisted. "Once this charm does its work and he loves me, you'll see. Everything will be wonderful." She fingered the charm again. "And when he does, there will be a bonus for you."

Olga shook her head. "You will need my help if you love that man."

Miranda glanced toward Piper and Jenny. A blush colored her delicate features. Olga followed the young woman's gaze.

"Tell your fortune?" Olga called to Piper and Jenny. She flicked her fingers at Miranda, clearly indicating that the woman should leave, now that new customers had arrived. Miranda scurried away.

Olga took a step toward them. "Come, see into the future. Come see Olga, who can tell all."

Jenny tugged Piper's hand. "Let's go."

Piper had hoped for a magic-free day. That's why she really wanted to come to the carnival.

"Want a curse removed? Bring bad luck to your enemy? Find out who is thinking of you? Olga the Gypsy Fortune-teller sees and knows all!"

Olga picked up a tambourine hanging by the door and began tapping it. It made a bright tinkling sound, but instantly sent Piper the message that the woman was a total scam artist. This should be an entirely magic-free zone, which would be all right with Piper. Besides, Jenny looked so eager. Consulting Olga would at least be entertaining.

"Okay," Piper said. "Go for it."

"Thank you!" Jenny ran up to Olga. "Can we see inside the wagon?"

"Ah, you like my *vardo?*" Olga asked. "That is the Gypsy word for our homes on wheels." She studied Jenny carefully. "For a Gypsy to invite a *gaujo* into her vardo, well, that requires great trust. The spirits are always about inside a vardo, and one does not like to disturb them. But yes . . . I believe you and your friend would be welcome."

"Cool!" Jenny turned to Piper. "Come on!"

I wonder what this is going to cost me, Piper thought. She figured the more elaborate the act, the higher the fee.

Piper followed Jenny and Olga into the vardo. Even in the dim light, she could see it was as colorfully decorated on the inside as it was on the outside. A pungent odor hung in the air; Olga must have been burning incense when she made Miranda's love charm, Piper figured.

A large kettle sat on the old-fashioned stove near the front. The area behind that curtain must be the sleeping quarters, Piper figured. The vardo was jammed with all manner of magical objects, along with pots, pans, dishes, and clothing. Herb bouquets hung drying in the windows, and jars filled with thick potions filled several shelves. Dust lay thick along counters, and the room seemed a bit smoky.

A small table covered with a black velvet cloth was set up in the middle of the room. A crystal ball sat in the center. Small seashells containing herbs and flower petals were arranged around the crystal ball. Piper assumed they were left over from the previous reading. She also spotted several decks of dog-eared cards sitting on the chair beside the table.

"Cross my palm with silver, and I shall tell you your future," Olga told Jenny. She sat the girl down in a chair at the table.

"Uh, how much silver?" Jenny asked uncertainly. She fiddled around with her fanny pack.

"My treat," Piper said. "So how much for a tarot card reading?"

Olga's eyes narrowed as she gazed at Piper's face.

She must be trying to figure out how much to charge. I hope I don't look too rich.

"Five dollars is the basic rate." Olga shrugged. "If required, we will go deeper."

Piper handed Olga a crisp five-dollar bill. Olga didn't take it from her right away. Instead, she and Piper stood for a moment clasping hands with the bill between their palms. Olga's eyes bored into Piper's. Piper felt uncomfortable under the momentary scrutiny. Almost instantly, Olga released her grip, smiled, and slipped the bill into her skirt pocket.

That was weird, Piper thought. She squeezed behind Jenny's chair, while Olga took her place at the opposite side of the table.

Olga reached out and took Jenny's hand. She studied it for a moment, then gazed into Jenny's eyes. "Ah, I see, yes. You would like to have some answers." She smiled, making her leathery face crinkle up into a network of wrinkles. "Maybe find out about your boyfriend?" Olga teased Jenny.

"I don't have a boyfriend," Jenny said, giggling.

"I knew that," Olga insisted. "I was just playing with the youngster."

Piper stifled a laugh. *Sure you knew that,* she thought. *And I know tomorrow's stock market picks.*

"What would you like to know, my child?" Olga asked.

"Um . . ." Jenny tilted her head to one side as she gave the question some thought. "I know!" She whirled around in her chair and peered up at Piper. "We can ask the cards about you and Dan." She turned back to Olga. "That's what I want to know. Will Piper and Dan get back together?"

Olga chose a pack of cards from the stack beside her. She shuffled them. "Ah. I see. We have a matter of broken hearts, eh?" Her eyes flicked up to Piper.

Piper crossed her arms over her chest and shook her head no. In case Olga missed her point, she pressed her fingers together in a prayer position and shook her head no again, even more emphatically.

Olga turned over a card. She clucked sympathetically. "Oh. Not a promising card for love," she said.

Piper breathed a tiny sigh of relief. Olga had gotten her silent message loud and clear.

"Isn't anything good going to happen?" Jenny asked.

Olga's eyes flicked again to Piper. Piper shrugged. She wasn't sure how Olga should answer that. But Olga was resourceful.

"Yes, of course," Olga said. "The good is that this relationship will finally be resolved. Both parties will find new loves."

Jenny frowned.

"Do you want to ask something for yourself?" Piper asked Jenny, giving the girl's slumped shoulders a quick squeeze. "We could try some other kind of reading." She hoped Olga would pick up on Jenny's disappointment and give the girl something more upbeat and fun to think about.

"I don't know . . ." Jenny muttered.

"The spirits are directing me," Olga announced. She pushed aside the cards and pulled the crystal ball toward her.

She waved her hands over it. "I see something through the mists." Her voice dropped down to a singsong whisper. She's an awfully good actress, Piper observed.

"Yes. Yes," Olga crooned. "There will be a great victory for you, young lady. Some positive outcome. A win of some kind. Is it a win in love? In a contest? In—"

"Is my soccer team going to win the tournament?" Jenny asked eagerly. She leaned forward, trying to peer into the crystal ball herself.

"If all things come to pass as they present themselves now, the answer is yes," Olga intoned.

Now, there's a nonanswer, Piper thought. She admired the clever way Olga gave an answer that would turn out to be correct no matter what happened.

It satisfied Jenny. "All right!" she cheered. "I knew we'd go all the way!"

"And we'd better go all the way to the circus tent," Piper noted. "The show is about to begin."

"Okay." Jenny stood. "Thank you," she told Olga.

"It is always a pleasure to read happy futures," Olga said.

Piper and Jenny left the dark booth. Piper blinked a few times, allowing her eyes to adjust to the bright light after the dim vardo.

She appreciated Olga picking up her cues. She decided to give the woman a tip. "Wait here," she instructed Jenny. "I just want to say something to Olga."

"Sure thing." Jenny replied. She started examining a shelf tacked up in one of the trees beside the wagon. It was filled with colorful scarves and doodads Olga had for sale outside.

Piper ducked back into the vardo. Olga's back was to her, but the woman stiffened. "I sense danger," Olga intoned.

She really gets into the act, doesn't she, Piper observed.

Olga turned. Piper was startled by the intensity in the woman's dark eyes.

Olga reached her hands out to Piper. "You must leave this place and never come back."

CHAPTER
4

Piper's eyes widened as she stared at the fortune-teller. The woman's ferocity was unmistakable.

Olga clutched the table edge. "Listen to me," she said to Piper. "You are in grave danger. The circus is not safe for you. Keep away."

"What do you mean?" Why would Olga want to scare me away from the carnival? Piper wondered. Or does she mean all circuses? Piper shook her head. "You have the wrong Halliwell," she said, trying to laugh it off. "My sister Prue is the one with the circus hang-up."

Olga sank down at the table. "All around you, I can sense an unusual energy field. It attracts darkness," she said.

Okay, I'm officially freaked out now, Piper thought. Could Olga actually be able to sense that I'm a witch? Piper wondered if the woman had what the Gypsies called "the gift of second sight."

Maybe the woman's act with Jenny wasn't bogus after all.

"There are evil forces at work at the Carnival Cavalcade," Olga said. "You see only pretty lights, hear the happy music. That is a mask to cover up the dark forces at work here. You must take great care."

"But how am I in danger?" Piper asked.

Olga shut her eyes. Her breath came in choking gasps. She let out a low moan. "A curse is afoot," she muttered. "It moves toward you." Olga's eyes popped open again. "That is all I can say. You must leave."

"Well, uh, thanks for the warning," Piper said. "I—I don't want to leave my friend alone."

Piper left Olga still moaning at the table. Once outside, Jenny beamed at her. "All set? We need to get to the tent."

"Great." Piper realized Olga had her so rattled that she had forgotten to leave the tip, only she didn't feel like going back in. Maybe I'll come back later, she told herself.

Piper tried to shake off the unsettled feeling as she and Jenny headed away from Olga's vardo. She felt as if someone was watching her. She glanced over her shoulder and saw Olga in front of her wagon, staring at Piper. When she caught Piper's eye, she lay a finger alongside her nose, made a gesture with her hand, and then hurried away toward the other trailers.

Okie-dokie, that was weird, Piper thought. I'll have to consult *The Book of Shadows* to see if it has anything to say about Gypsy magic. Could Olga actually have seen in those cards that I'm a witch?

And what was all that about a curse headed my way?

Piper shook her head. Whatever. She decided to steer clear of Olga. The fortune-teller seemed to have been quite affected by what she thought—or was pretending to think, Piper reminded herself—might happen to Piper. Still, better not to upset the woman. More important, if the woman had actual powers, Piper didn't want Olga to figure out that she was a witch.

Prue gazed at Ivan the Gypsy Violinist through the viewfinder of her camera and clicked. Another perfect shot. This guy doesn't have a bad angle, she thought. He's that drop-dead gorgeous.

Kristin was perched on the small built-in bed in Ivan's trailer, taking notes. They had been interviewing Ivan for the last hour, and as far as Prue was concerned, time was just flying.

"This is your second season with the carnival," Kristin said. "What were you doing before that?"

"I was performing with smaller circuses in Europe," Ivan replied. "Mr. Amalfi had heard of me and very kindly offered me a headliner spot with the Carnival Cavalcade."

Kristin flipped open a folder she had balanced on her lap. She riffled through the press clippings. "You're being much too modest," she scolded Ivan. "According to Mr. Amalfi, you were on your way to becoming a huge European star, and he was lucky enough to snatch you up."

Ivan ducked his head, sending his thick dark curls cascading across his broad forehead. "He is too kind."

Ivan got up and crossed over to the small kitchen area. He held up a box of tea. "Would you care for any?" he asked Prue and Kristin.

"No thanks," Kristin said as Prue shook her head no. Ivan filled a tea kettle with water from the tiny sink and set it on a hot plate.

Prue marveled at how nice the trailer was. Compact, yes, she thought, eyeing the mini-fridge, the built-in bed, and the skinny door to the bathroom, but colorful and clean. There didn't seem to be a single inch of unused space. Prue knew she wanted to get shots of the interior: The magazine's readers would definitely be curious about how a circus performer lived, although any picture without Ivan in it seemed like a waste of film.

Luckily, I can stare at him all I want, Prue thought with a grin. I'm the photographer.

She studied Ivan through the camera. He had high, prominent cheekbones and olive-tone skin. His enormous dark eyes were almond shaped with thick lashes. Why do guys always get the great lashes? she thought ruefully, while we girls have to load on the mascara.

Ivan wore a midnight blue and silver scarf tied though his thick mop of unruly curls like a runner's sweatband. His tight black pants reminded Prue of those worn by bullfighters, while the white gauzy shirt with billowing sleeves and the high suede boots made Ivan look like a pirate. The small silver hoop in his ear added to the effect.

Prue realized that as she was scrutinizing Ivan, he was watching her. "It is a shame to cover such a pretty face," Ivan said to Prue.

"What?" She lowered the camera.

Ivan smiled, revealing two adorable dimples. "Much better. Now I can see you."

Prue smiled back. And I wanted to bag this assignment? Was I nuts? "I have to do my job, you know."

"Ah, well, then I suppose if you must, you must."

Kristin eyed them with amusement. "If you two could stop flirting for a minute, I'd like to finish up this interview."

Prue knew that Kristin loved nothing better than romance—she'd heard enough of Kristin's endless attempts to fix up her friends. Then Prue also remembered how much Kristin enjoyed gossip. Better concentrate on work or the rumors would be flying at 415 before she had time to develop her film.

"Your colleague is right, of course," Ivan said. "Work is important. Discipline. But so is pleasure."

This time work is definitely a pleasure, Prue thought, patting her camera.

"I know in your act you're billed as Ivan the Gypsy Violinist," Kristin said. She leaned toward Ivan and her voice became low and conspiratorial. "Tell me. Are you really a Gypsy?" She gave Ivan a sly grin. "Or is that just for publicity because it makes you seem exotic?"

"No, I am true Romany," Ivan declared. "Rom or Romany is the accurate term for my people. There are many tribes still scattered throughout the world. My family traveled primarily in Eastern Europe. But we share language with the Rom in many countries, from England to Romania to Mongolia. The Rom have always traveled, though not always by choice."

Prue wondered if Ivan's Gypsy heritage had fostered the rumors about his bad luck. She knew Gypsies were associated with all kinds of magic. Curses, divination, and the reading of signs and omens were the dark skills Prue thought of when she heard the word *Gypsy*.

"What do you think about Gypsy curses?" Prue wanted to see if he had heard the rumors about him. Sacha, the Man-in-the-Moon clown, had made it seem as if Ivan's "curse" was common knowledge.

His dark eyes darkened further. "I have of course heard these things." He seemed upset by the question.

"So I guess you believe them," Prue said.

"No, you misunderstand." Ivan ran his hands through his thick hair. Prue found herself wishing she could do the same thing. Those curls were adorable.

"The Gypsies have been persecuted for centuries because of such beliefs," Ivan explained. "They have been accused of witchcraft and burned."

Gee. So we have something in common after all, Prue thought. That's been the fate of some of my relatives, too. But Prue stayed silent, of course.

The kettle whistled and Ivan made his tea. "In my family we have great pride in our heritage, but don't go for all that hocus-pocus." He brought his teacup over to the small table that flipped out of the wall. "I think it's one of the reasons we Gypsies have had so many hard times. The believers think we are doing the work of demons. The nonbelievers think we are childish for our occult practices, even if we don't practice anything of the sort."

"That *is* tough," Kristin said sympathetically.

You don't know the half of it, Prue thought. I can really relate. She switched cameras. The thoughtfulness on Ivan's face would be better captured in black and white.

"Besides, I don't believe any of it. My family stayed away from all that. Personally, I think the so-called Gypsy magic is just a ruse to separate the gaujos from their money."

"Gaujos?" Kristin asked.

"It's a Rom term for non-Gypsies."

Kristin took a note while Ivan cast Prue a sidelong glance. Prue felt herself flush under his gaze. She was glad she could hide behind her camera. This guy was having a major effect on her.

Kristin bit the eraser tip of her pencil. "Now I don't want you to take offense," she said sweetly. "But I guess what you're saying is that there are some Gypsy fortune-tellers who, well, sort of rip people off. You know"—she lowered her voice and glanced around as if she didn't want anyone to over-hear her—"not totally honest."

Prue shook her head. How anyone so uncomfort-able with asking hard questions as Kristin ever chose journalism was beyond her. Of course, it suddenly occurred to her, Kristin's sweetness-and-light act could be just that—an act. She did manage to soften up some seriously tough interview subjects.

"Please don't quote me as saying that," Ivan answered. He laughed. "I probably have distant cousins in that very trade."

"Well, of course, not anyone in your own immedi-ate family!" Kristin exclaimed as if horrified that

Ivan might imagine she would suggest anything of the sort.

"My tribe had two areas of expertise," Ivan said. "Many Gypsy families specialize in specific skills. Some are smiths, working in metal, some are cobblers, some are horse breeders. Others concentrate on performing, like my family."

Prue enjoyed Ivan's obvious pride in his family's history. She, too, felt a bond with her own family traditions, particularly since she knew her magic was something that had been passed down to her and her sisters through their ancestors. *I guess we Halliwells have gone into the family business—only our family business is witchcraft.*

"Has your family always been in the circus?" Kristin asked, scribbling away.

"On my father's side," Ivan said. "Always working with the animals. On my mother's side, the family has made instruments. I have melded the two together."

Ivan stood and in two steps crossed to an ornately painted cabinet. He unlocked the doors and pulled out a decorated violin case. "This has been in my family for several generations," he explained. He flipped open the case and carefully removed a well-polished violin. The instrument gleamed, obviously from the loving attention that had been paid to it over the years.

Ivan gently cradled the violin. "My mother's father's father made this. Her father made the case. Now I play the violin in my act."

"What is your act, exactly?" Prue asked. "Sorry, but I don't go to the circus much. I know you're world famous and everything . . ."

Ivan smiled at her. "I take no offense. The circus is a special place. Not everyone feels its pull."

"Maybe you'll change my mind," Prue said.

"I hope I will," Ivan replied, his dark eyes filled with warmth.

"Ivan does an amazing act with animals," Kristin gushed. "It's brilliant. Gorgeous. Spectacular." She took in a deep breath and shivered with delight.

"You've seen it?" Prue asked her.

She nodded. "In Europe. It's beautiful." She gazed at Ivan adoringly. "You are the main reason I worked really hard to pitch this story."

"Thank you, but it is too much." Ivan turned back to Prue. "My animals and I enjoy the music of my violin together. That is all."

Kristin laughed. "You say it as if it's nothing! Prue, he gets tigers and lions and bears to dance. And the music! I've never forgotten it."

"I play the songs of my people," Ivan said. "Old folk songs from my childhood. The melodies are very rich."

"I can't wait to see you perform," Prue said. To her surprise, she actually meant it.

Ivan laid the violin back in its case and returned it to the cabinet. Then he stood and turned, opening his arms wide.

"Now you must see my costars," he declared. "I am nothing without them."

"Oh, could we?" Kristin squealed.

"That will make great pictures," Prue said, adopting a more professional stance. Somebody had to.

Ivan led Kristin and Prue back through the maze of trailers, deeper into the parklands. Some of Golden Gate Park was pretty wild.

And getting wilder. Prue could smell the animals before she saw them. Her nose wrinkled at the pungent, earthy odor. Low growls and rumbling sounds came through the trees.

"Ahh," Ivan said softly. "They know we are coming. They are calling to us."

Ivan brought Prue and Kristin into a clearing ringed with large metal cages. Inside each one animals paced, and Prue's pulse quickened. To be near all that pure animal power and energy, there was something thrilling about it.

Ivan began to hum a haunting melody. The animals seemed to recognize it. They stopped pacing and sat patiently in the centers of their cages. They looked expectantly at Ivan.

Ivan bounded over to the cages, as lighthearted as a puppy. "Come join me!" he called to Prue and Kristin. He waved them into the center of the clearing.

"Hello." Ivan reached into the cage to pet an enormous tiger. The tiger sloppily licked Ivan's arm. "Miss me? Ready to show off? We have some pretty ladies we want to impress."

Kristin giggled. "Hi, kitty," she said. Prue was afraid the overjoyed journalist would swoon with delight right on the spot. Prue could tell Kristin had no romantic interest in Ivan; nor was she the investigative reporter right now. The woman was simply a heartfelt fan.

"The animals love you," Prue observed.

"The feeling is mutual." Ivan moved over to the bears. One of them reached through the bar, playfully cuffing Ivan. Ivan didn't seemed fazed at all.

"It's the only way it can work," Ivan explained, giving a large black bear a much-enjoyed scratch behind the ear. "We love each other, and more important, we respect each other."

Ivan wove in and out of the cages, speaking softly to each of the animals in turn. He never used any kind of force, even when the lion got feisty and needed some persuasion to release Ivan's shirt from its claws.

"Are you all right?" Prue asked, trying not to stare with horror at Ivan's shredded sleeve. All she kept thinking was that it could have been his arm in pieces.

"He's just being himself," Ivan said. "You can't expect an animal to be anything other than an animal. They are beautiful creatures—noble and pure. If one is lucky enough to have a special relationship with them, as I have, one is truly blessed."

Prue watched Ivan check each animal's paws and ears, replenish their food, speaking softly to each one, stroking their fur.

What a gentle, caring man he is. She sighed. Not to mention seriously handsome.

A movement in the bushes caught Prue's attention. Kristin was so caught up with Ivan that she didn't notice. Only the lion seemed to be aware they were being watched.

A thick, heavy-set woman wearing colorful clothes stood staring at them.

Prue went over to Ivan. "Who is that?" she whispered. She nodded toward the bushes.

Ivan glanced over. Then he went back to grooming the bear cub. "That's Olga."

"She looks angry," Prue commented.

"Olga the fortune-teller?" Kristin asked. She shaded her eyes from the bright sun, trying to make out Olga in the bushes. "She's on my interview list, too. Can you introduce me?"

A dark look crossed Ivan's handsome features. "Better not to meet her through me."

"Why not?" Prue asked. "Are you from rival Gypsy families or something?"

"Not exactly," Ivan said. "Though we don't see eye to eye on several subjects."

Prue glanced back at Olga. The woman was muttering and making strange hand gestures. "What is she doing?" Prue asked Ivan.

"She is protecting herself from the evil eye," Ivan replied grimly. "She wants to be sure she doesn't catch the curse she believes is on my head."

CHAPTER 5

A curse! Fabulous!" Kristin gushed. "That will make such wonderful human interest."

"No!" Ivan snapped.

Prue's head whipped around to stare at Ivan. It was the first time she had heard him raise his voice. Even when the lion insisted on shredding his shirt sleeve, and the bear tossed its food out of the cage at him, Ivan didn't yell.

"You mustn't write about the curse," he ordered. Prue was surprised by the hardness that had appeared in his deep-set eyes.

Kristin was oblivious to Ivan's change of mood—or was pretending to be. "Why not? It will make a great story."

"I don't want the world laughing at the foolish Gypsies," Ivan insisted. "Curses, superstition, it is all ridiculous. Olga talks of signs and portents. Old-fashioned nonsense."

Prue studied Ivan carefully. This was the second time today someone had hinted that he was cursed. She had not seen any ill effects around him, but wondered if perhaps there was truth to the rumors.

"Let us go back," Ivan said, obviously wanting to change the subject. "It is time for me to prepare." He held up his arm so that the shredded sleeve dangled. He grinned, breaking the tension of the moment. "You have no idea how many shirts I go through."

"I can imagine," Kristin said, laughing. "The wholesaler must love you."

Prue hung back, gazing at the gorgeous animals. "Listen, you go on ahead," she told them. "The light is beautiful right now. I'd like to get some more pictures."

A look of concern crossed Ivan's face. "I generally do not allow anyone near my animals without me," he said.

"I promise to stay back," Prue said. "And I won't antagonize them in any way."

Ivan still didn't look quite convinced. "People see the way they are with me and believe the animals are tame. They are not. They will rip apart a stranger as any wild beast would."

Prue nodded. "I understand. It's that essence I'd like to try to capture, actually. The contrast between their behavior on their own and their behavior with you."

Ivan studied her a moment longer, then said, "I believe you do understand. Respect their power. It is different from yours and mine."

"That's a great idea for shots," Kristin said. "I just knew you'd be perfect for this assignment." She gave first Prue and then Ivan a sly glance. "Isn't she perfect?" she asked Ivan in a very leading tone.

Prue shook her head at the obvious matchmaking attempt. "Go," she said. "I don't want the light to change."

Prue spent some time taking pictures of Ivan's animal partners. They were different when he was around. Alone with them, Prue was very aware that she was among creatures unlike herself. No matter how much she might think of them as big versions of pussycats, they weren't. The lions and tigers stared at her with mysterious eyes making her realize that she would never quite grasp what was going on inside them. She could never truly enter their world.

She finished the roll of film, then checked her watch.

"Oops," Prue said. "Don't want to be late for the show." Prue packed up her equipment and headed back toward the main part of the carnival.

Soon enough she recognized Ivan's trailer. She rapped lightly on the door, but there wasn't any answer. He and Kristin must have gone on to the show, she figured. Prue picked up speed and caught her heel in the gravel.

"Oh, darn these sandals." Prue bent down to try to fix the flimsy shoe. A strange shadow appeared on the ground in front of her.

"Ruby," a raspy voice said.

Prue's eyes traveled up to see who had spoken. She wobbled a little in her crouched position.

That is some wicked costume, Prue thought.

The guy wore tattered rags, and the hands that hung below his torn sleeves were long and skeletal.

His face was a ghastly greenish yellow, and his eyes seemed to be just gaping sockets. He looked as if his skin were peeling off its skull. What an amazing makeup job, Prue observed.

"Ruby?" he croaked again.

Prue stood unsteadily. "No, I'm not Ruby."

The guy wavered a moment, as though Prue's words confused him, then he shuffled away, back behind Ivan's trailer.

Prue stood staring after him. Do all the performers stay in character the way those clowns did this morning?

Another thought occurred to her. Why would such a ghastly character be part of this sunny circus? A figure like that would terrify kids.

Maybe he wasn't a performer, she realized, her stomach starting to twist. Maybe he has something to do with Ivan's so-called curse.

Before she could investigate further, Kristin bounced over to her. "There you are! Come on! The show's about to start. We don't want to miss a single minute!"

"Okay," Prue murmured. She shivered. Ivan may not believe in signs and portents, but perhaps he should.

Phoebe scrunched down in the hard chair as low as she could. She wished she had a hat she could pull down over her face, or better yet, a total disguise. Anything to get Raphael the Tattooed Snake-Charmer off her trail.

Why is it that I'm irresistible to creeps? Phoebe wondered. When Piper attracts a guy, he's someone hunky and sweet like Dan or Leo. She has two fabulous men fighting over her and I've got what? A wacko who comes with his very own boa constrictor.

Not that it's so easy to have to choose, Phoebe knew. Watching Piper struggle with the Dan-Leo triangle wasn't pretty. Phoebe hoped her sister was handling that accidental meeting with Dan. That was so not on the agenda. Things are always so sticky around Dan. Piper still had really strong feelings for him, and it was way obvious that Dan's little heart was pit-a-patting over Piper. Still, Phoebe figured they were both being very adult about it all, especially since Jenny was around as a witness. Phoebe sighed. She hoped this wouldn't stir up those doubts for Piper. It had been such hard work for her, figuring out the right thing to do.

Phoebe shifted in the uncomfortable seat. Hmm. These free passes didn't exactly land us in the VIP section, did they, she observed. More like nosebleed section. Phoebe's seat was up near the back wall of the tent, far from the ring. She wasn't complaining, though. She still had a great view. She could even see Prue down at ringside, snapping away.

Music blared from the loudspeakers, and clowns tumbled in the aisles, stealing hats and tossing balloons. The candy sellers shouted their wares.

"Over here!" Phoebe called. She waved over a popcorn seller. As far as Phoebe was concerned, one of the best things about carnivals and circuses was that you had an excuse to eat all the junk food you wanted. It was practically a requirement! She handed the teenager her money and accepted an enormous

box of popcorn. She craned her neck, scanning the
tent for the hundredth time. Now, where was Piper?
What could be taking her so long?

Just as Phoebe was ready to get up to start a
search, Piper and Jenny arrived.

"Hey, guys," Phoebe said. "I thought maybe one
of the elephants had stomped you."

"Nope. Just distracted," Piper replied.

Phoebe couldn't read her sister. No time to find
out how things had gone with Dan. His noticeable
absence, however, spoke volumes.

"So just us girls?" Phoebe said with a raised ques-
tioning eyebrow.

"Yup," Piper said.

"This is so babyish," Jenny complained. "I can't
believe Dan thought I'd want to go to the dumb old
circus. I mean, who thinks clowns are funny except
little kids."

"I do, for one," Phoebe said. She wondered if
Jenny's crankiness had to do with the failed romance
between Dan and Piper.

However, as the circus got under way, Phoebe
watched in amusement as Jenny's demeanor changed.
The girl was at the edge of her seat for the aerialists
and gasped at Miranda Merrill, tightrope walker
extraordinaire. She even laughed at the antics of the
clowns. When the elephants stole the jugglers' clubs,
Phoebe thought Jenny might actually collapse, she
was guffawing so hard.

"Ladies and gentlemen, children of all ages!" the
ringmaster's voice boomed over the loudspeaker.
"For our next act, I ask that you be as quiet as possible. For you will be entertained not only by amazing

wild beasts, but also by the beautiful music of Ivan the Gypsy Violinist!"

The lights went down. A hush fell over the tent. Out of the darkness a tiger's loud growl was heard. It was taken up by the roar of a lion, and then the sounds of bears snuffling and growling. Jenny grabbed Phoebe's hand. Phoebe noticed the girl was also clutching Piper's hand.

Above the growing animal sounds came a pure note, high and sweet. Instantly Jenny's grip lessened. As the note became a lilting melody, the lights came up on a tall man in the center of the ring. He was playing the violin. He wore a billowing white shirt and tight black pants. Circling the ring were animal cages. The roustabouts must have moved them into place in the dark.

Now the violinist began to dance as he played. He did some steps over to the lion's cage. With a twist and a kick, he flicked open the cage with his foot.

Serious Tae-Bo action, Phoebe thought admiringly. Actually, she decided, more Riverdance than martial arts.

The violinist continued to dance around the ring, kicking open cages. He never stopped playing. The melody soared and dipped. It sounded both familiar yet completely new. Nothing else could be heard in the ring; even the animals seemed mesmerized.

Once all the cages were open, the violinist returned to the center of the ring. He played a new song, and now the animals joined him in the dance. A tiger stood on its hind legs, placed its heavy paws on the violinist's shoulders, taking care not to dislodge the violin. They whirled around the ring together. The lions paced in time to the music, dipping their heads in unison to the beat. The bears chased each other, pulling pranks on Ivan as if they were naughty children. Then they rolled around on the ground as if they were laughing.

All the time the violinist played. Phoebe didn't want the music ever to stop. She glanced around the tent. The entire audience seemed to be entranced. They smiled at one another, complete strangers holding hands and grinning. A sense of well-being permeated the tent.

Each of the animals was given a special moment to shine. The bears were adorable—clumsy but endearing. The lions were dramatic, the tigers majestic.

Finally, the violinist played the last notes. All the animals took a bow. Then, as he played an exit march, each animal trooped back into its cage. The violinist once more stood alone in the center of the ring, played a single note, and the lights blinked out.

For a moment the entire tent was silent, as if the audience didn't know what to do now that the music had stopped. Then as if a button had been pushed, thunderous applause filled the tent.

"That was beautiful," Jenny gasped. Her eyes were shining, as if she was about to cry.

Phoebe found herself feeling a bit choked up herself. But then, I'm a total sucker for guys in tights with gorgeous animals—not to mention serious animal magnetism.

The clowns tumbled back into the ring, changing the pace of the show. After the mesmerizing performance of Ivan the Gypsy Violinist, the clowns' antics were a welcome change. Their pranks seemed even funnier now—or maybe everyone was in such a good mood after Ivan's lovely act that anything the clowns did would be A-OK with them, Phoebe observed.

All too soon the entire cast appeared for the final parade. The circus band played lively music as the ringmaster and the clowns got the entire audience clapping and stomping its feet. Then the show was over.

"That was awesome!" Jenny exclaimed.

"Not too babyish?" Piper asked with a smile.

"Not at all! This was totally great!"

"I thought so, too!" Piper gave Jenny a quick hug.

"Now do we get to go meet the performers?" Jenny asked.

"We'll see," Piper said. "We do get to go down to the ring and find Prue. There will probably be performers around. Maybe we'll be able to wrangle some introductions."

"I want to meet the Gypsy violinist," Jenny said. "And I want to pet one of those cute little pigs that chased the clowns."

"Okay," Piper said, tucking the program into her purse.

"Hurry!" Jenny urged. "I don't want to miss this chance!"

Piper rolled her eyes good-naturedly at Phoebe. "This from a girl who claimed she didn't want to be here."

Phoebe stood up. "Oops!" Phoebe's purse tumbled from her lap. Unfortunately the drawstring top wasn't very secure and out rolled a lipstick, a pen, and a mascara wand.

She knelt down as Jenny hurried Piper along the bleachers and down toward the ring. Phoebe tossed her stuff back into her cloth bag and gave the drawstring an extra-hard tug. She stood back up and spotted the sweater Piper had left draped over her seat. "I guess the circus got us all in a bit of a daze," she muttered.

She reached for the soft peach-colored sleeve. A startling shock of energy surged through her.

The bustling circus tent vanished as a powerful vision took hold of Phoebe. Images flooded through her.

Large powerful hands gripping a slim neck.

Smaller hands desperately clawing at those hands.

Long hair swirling in the struggle.

Huge brown eyes filled with cruelty and fury.

Pain. Terror. No air. Can't breathe.

Phoebe released the sweater. It fell between the bleachers. She steadied herself by gripping the back of a seat.

Piper. Her vision was of Piper being strangled by a handsome stranger.

CHAPTER
6

Phoebe took in several deep breaths to center herself. It always took a few seconds to recover from one of her visions. They came on so powerfully, took her over, and left her a little disoriented.

She needed to keep a clear head. She had to get Piper out of there—fast. The tricky part was to do so without giving anything away in front of Jenny.

Phoebe hurried down the bleachers toward the ring. She ducked past kids crowding around a merry clown. Other children were being ushered out by their parents. Roustabouts were already sweeping the ring, getting ready to set up for the next show a few hours later.

Phoebe stood on one of the bleachers, eyeing the crowded backstage area. Several security guards were patrolling, barking into walkie-talkies.

Where are they? Phoebe scanned for Piper. The problem with her visions was that she never had any idea how much time she had before the future she had flashed on came to pass. Was Piper being strangled this minute? It was such chaos down by ringside. It was easy to imagine someone snatching her sister and dragging her behind some trailer and leaving her for dead.

Why hadn't the vision been clearer? All Phoebe had been able to see was the hatred in the handsome man's eyes and his hands squeezing the life out of Piper. There had been no indication of where this horrible attack would take place. No clothing clues. No sense of time of day. Just the cruelly handsome face, Piper's terror and gasps for breath, and her desperate attempt to escape from the powerful grip around her throat.

"Piper!" Phoebe called, scanning the area. Then relief flooded through her. There was Piper, talking animatedly with Jenny. The only guy nearby did not qualify as handsome by anyone's standards: Raphael the snake charmer.

The way Jenny was peering around the stands made Phoebe suspect that Raphael was asking Jenny where she was. Should I hide? Can't. Gotta get Piper out of here, grab Prue, and call a Halliwell powwow pronto.

I hope Piper appreciates this, Phoebe thought as she made a beeline toward the little group. Volunteering to put myself into Raphael's orbit really is going above and beyond.

At least Ralphie-boy was minus the snake, Phoebe noted. Only she wondered if maybe she'd prefer the reptile's company. Ralph was far more slithery and certainly slimier.

"Pretty lady, I've been looking all over for you," Raphael said to Phoebe. He grinned, displaying a gold canine tooth. "Not that you gals aren't lookers yourself," he added to Piper and Jenny.

"Well, you found me. And now we have to disappear. Piper?" Phoebe grabbed Piper's arm. One good thing about Raphael's presence: Jenny might assume they were escaping from Raphael's not-too-charming charms and not Phoebe's attempt to prevent a murder predicted by a supernatural vision.

"Why, Phoebe, you said you wanted to meet some circus guys," Piper said, stifling a giggle. "What's your rush? Isn't Raphael your type?"

"We need to find Prue and get going, sister dear," Phoebe said through gritted teeth. How could she warn Piper with Jenny standing right there? Too bad our powers don't include telepathy.

"I don't want to go," Jenny complained. "I want to meet the performers." She glared at Piper. "And you promised that after the show we could try out all the games on the midway."

Piper looked appealingly to Phoebe. "Well, I did prom—"

Phoebe cut her off. "Another time. Piper, we have that really important thingie. Don't you remember?"

Piper looked puzzled. "What kind of thingie?"

"Something I *saw* . . . and then because I *saw* it, I got really interested . . ."

Phoebe could see the light dawn in her sister's eyes.

"Oh, right!" Piper slapped her forehead. "The thingie."

"What thingie?" Jenny asked.

Piper stared at Phoebe. "Uh, Phoebe?"

Phoebe thought fast. What could she say they had to do that Jenny wouldn't want to tag along for? Something a twelve-year-old would find boring.

"I saw some excellent new tires that I thought we should buy, and they had just gone on sale," Phoebe said. "We need to get there before the store closes."

Jenny looked baffled. "You want to leave without meeting anyone for that?" she asked. Then she seemed to remember her manners. "Well, okay . . ." She dropped her chin and gazed down at the ground. "If you really have to."

Phoebe gave a decisive nod. "We really have to. Now, where's Prue?"

"I'm not really sure," Piper told her. "She said she wanted to check on something with a costumer. Maybe she's setting up a shoot in the wardrobe trailer."

"There she is." Jenny pointed toward a stack of props.

Phoebe turned and saw her sister talking to a short, stylish woman with cropped hair who was holding several clothing hangers. Prue's expression was concerned, perplexed. I don't know what's bothering her right now, Phoebe thought, but once I tell her about the vision she'll be even more worried.

The woman with Prue vanished back among the crew. Prue glanced around. Phoebe waved at her, and Prue came over to join them. "Hi, what's up?" Prue asked.

"Tire shopping," Jenny said in a voice dripping with disappointment.

"What?" Prue's eyes darted back and forth between her sisters.

"You know me," Phoebe said brightly. "Once I *see* something, I just have to act on it immediately. So let's get out of here!"

Prue seemed to pick up the message. Despite having been the Charmed Ones for a while, Phoebe noticed, we're only just starting to get our secret codes down. We really need to come up with a signal or a code or a handshake or something so we don't have to go through all this. After all, we spend an awful lot of time trying to discuss things that can't be discussed in front of other people.

Kristin charged over. "Ready?" she asked Prue.

Uh-oh, Phoebe thought. How is Prue going to get out of here? She's supposed to be working.

"Actually, Kristin, something's come up," Prue said. "An emergency."

Kristin's face clouded with concern. "What kind of emergency? Is everything okay?" She held up a hand to stop Prue from answering. "I'm sorry, I don't mean to get personal. You do what you need to do."

Phoebe was impressed. Kristin was being really cool about Prue taking off. The reporter's famous niceness was making it almost too easy. Even Phoebe was beginning to feel guilty about lying to the woman. And Phoebe knew what was at stake.

"Thanks, Kristin," Prue said gratefully. "I promise I'll be set for a full day tomorrow."

"Bright and early then," Kristin said. "I'll give you a list of anything from this afternoon you should shoot."

She squeezed Prue's shoulder. "Isn't this the greatest assignment! You can thank me later! Toodles!" She rushed away.

"Did she say 'toodles'?" Jenny asked, staring after Kristin.

"She also says 'gee whiz,' " Prue replied.

"Are the tires an emergency?" Jenny asked.

"They will be if we have a flat," Phoebe said. "Let's go."

Phoebe hurried them to the parking lot. She practically had them jogging. Once they got into the car Jenny asked, "Is something wrong? You're all being kind of weird."

Uh-oh. Better do something to distract her, Phoebe thought. She turned around in the front seat to face Jenny in the back. "We *are* weird," Phoebe joked. "You only just noticed that?"

Jenny's forehead crinkled. "No, really. Did I do something?"

"No sweetie, of course not." Piper hugged Jenny and looked at Phoebe. Phoebe read her sister's message loud and clear. We need to get on to some interesting topic fast.

"So what did you think of the circus?" Phoebe asked. "Not for babies, after all?

Jenny leaned back against the car seat. "Nope. I guess I actually have to thank Uncle Dan for setting this up, after all." She smiled at Piper. "It was a hundred times better hanging out with you, though."

"What was your favorite part?" Phoebe asked, keeping Jenny occupied.

Jenny thought for a moment. "Everything," she declared.

"Even Raphael the snake charmer?" Piper teased.

Jenny made a face and laughed. "Okay, not everything. Besides, he's Phoebe's boyfriend." She reached between the front seats and poked Phoebe in the side. "I don't want to steal him away from her."

"Ha. Ha." Phoebe said, trying to grab Jenny's finger. "Very funny."

"My favorite was Ivan the Gypsy Violinist," Piper said.

"That was something special all right," Phoebe agreed.

"Did you and Kristin interview him?" Piper asked.

"Yes," Prue said.

Phoebe could tell by the way Prue was biting her lip, trying to keep the enormous grin from spreading across her face, that this Ivan had made an impact on her big sister. Phoebe suspected the whammy had happened up close and personal and was not simply based on his expertise in the ring. "And . . . ?" Phoebe said.

"And he's very . . . interesting."

Phoebe knew there was more to this story. "Spill, sis. I haven't seen you blush since I don't know when."

Prue shook her head, grinning. "Can't get anything by you, can I? Okay. So I liked him. He's very charming."

Piper and Jenny both leaned forward. "What does this charmer look like?" Piper asked. "We couldn't see him very clearly from our seats."

"Is he handsome?" Jenny asked. Phoebe had a feeling Piper would be relieved that Jenny was interested in a romance other than Piper and Dan's. Talking about Ivan was an excellent distraction on a number of levels.

" 'Handsome' doesn't describe it," Prue said, giving Jenny a smile in the rearview mirror. "But he's also smart, levelheaded, and very interesting."

"Is he really a Gypsy?" Phoebe asked, hoping to continue this line of conversation.

"Yes."

"Does he know Gypsy magic?" Jenny asked. "Can he tell fortunes?"

"He doesn't believe in that stuff," Prue said. Phoebe couldn't tell from Prue's tone if Ivan didn't believe in magic or if she wanted to keep Jenny off the tricky subject.

"He did tell me a lot of Gypsy folklore, though," Prue added.

"Cool," Jenny said. "Like what?"

Phoebe listened with amusement as Prue described different kinds of Gypsy love spells.

"Ooh, so he's telling you all about love tokens," Piper teased. "Must be so you'll recognize them if he sends them your way."

Prue scrunched up her face at Piper in the rearview mirror. Piper scrunched back.

"What else?" Jenny asked eagerly.

Phoebe began to relax a little. This conversation certainly occupied Jenny's attention and as long as they were in the car, Piper was in no danger. Still, Phoebe was eager to get home so that they could get to work on preventing her horrible premonition.

"Let's see," Prue said, carefully threading her way through traffic. "There's a legend about a magical jewel called the Romany ruby. Supposedly, it gives the gypsy who has it—how did he put it? Oh yes, threefold power. The story goes that it returned to the astral plane to renew its power after its last owner died. Ivan said tribes have turned against one another over this gem."

"Wow. Sounds intense," Piper said.

Prue stopped at a red light. "Ivan doesn't believe the gem actually exists. In fact, the interfamily fighting over trying to recall it from the astral plane is one of the reasons Ivan's parents turned away from Gypsy lore."

"You're right," Piper said. "He does sound level-headed."

Phoebe began getting antsy again. Would this traffic ever let up? She used every ounce of self-control to keep from blurting out the news of her premonition. But she was grateful that all this talk of Ivan and legends kept Jenny from asking anything more about their hasty departure from the Carnival Cavalcade.

Jenny let out a sigh, a dreamy expression on her face. "It's all so romantic. And his music is so beautiful."

"There are even stories about his violin," Prue continued, pulling back into traffic. "It's been handed down through generations. And there is a belief that the violin chooses its owner."

"How does the violin do that?" Jenny asked.

"When it's time to pass it on, each child is allowed to play it. The violin will sing its choice."

"It sings?" Phoebe asked. Despite her anxiety, she found herself caught up in Ivan's colorful stories.

"Ivan doesn't believe there's anything supernatural at work," Prue explained. "The way Ivan sees it, the kid with innate musical abilities is the one who gets the instrument. That way Mom and Dad aren't subjected to all those years of torturous violin screeching. Pretty story with a basis in pragmatic fact."

"That spoils it," Jenny complained. "I like it better the other way."

"Well, here we are," Phoebe announced as Prue pulled up into the Halliwells' driveway. She scrambled out of the car quickly. "Gotta hurry, girls," she ordered. "Don't want to miss out on the best tire deals!"

"Thanks for a great day! I'll see you tomorrow." Jenny hugged Piper. "Have fun tire shopping."

The three Halliwells waved at Jenny as the twelve-year-old dashed toward her house.

"Okay, Phoebe," Piper demanded, a smile still plastered on her face. "What did you see?"

Jenny turned, waved, and popped into her house. Piper, Prue, and Phoebe spun on their heels and raced up the walk.

Prue unlocked the door. "You had a vision, right? That's what caused this sudden need for tires?"

"Affirmative," Phoebe said, hurrying inside. She was so relieved to have the chance finally to say what had been bottled up inside her that she had nervous energy to spare. She charged into the living room, whirled around, and pointed at Piper. "Piper. Getting strangled."

Piper sank onto the couch. "Oooh-kay. By whom?"

Phoebe paced around the living room. "No one I'd ever seen before."

"Demon? Warlock?" Prue pressed.

Phoebe shook her head. "He looked human. Filled with demonic fury, maybe, but a man."

"That narrows it down," Piper muttered. "Stay away from men. Actually, that would make my life a lot simpler anyway."

"Good-looking men," Phoebe added.

A look of panic crossed Piper's face. "It wasn't Leo or Dan, was it?"

"No," Phoebe assured her sister. "I told you—I didn't recognize him."

Piper leaned against the back of the couch. Prue sat down beside her. "So total trolls only," Piper said. "Fine by me."

"This is serious," Phoebe scolded. "I have no clue where, when, or why this is going to happen."

"Prue, you've been unnaturally silent," Piper commented.

"I'm just wondering . . ." Prue stood up again and gazed out the window.

Piper and Phoebe exchanged a glance. "Yeah?" Phoebe said, encouraging Prue to continue.

Prue crossed her arms over her chest. "I saw someone—or *something*—strange by Ivan's trailer just before the show," she said.

"A good-looking strangler," Piper stated.

Prue turned and looked at her sisters. She shook her head. "Good-looking this guy was not. I wondered if maybe he was a costumed performer, but when I described him, no one seemed to know who I was talking about."

Phoebe listened as Prue described the tattered outfit and the decaying face. "That is definitely not the guy in my vision."

"You know," Piper said slowly. "That costume sounds like traditional Gypsy gear. I saw pictures of men dressed like that in Olga the fortune-teller's wagon. None of them had hollow eyes and dripping flesh, though," she added.

Phoebe noticed a glint of surprise in Prue's blue eyes. "You met Olga?" she asked Piper.

Piper nodded and plopped a pillow onto her lap. "Jenny insisted on finding out if there was any hope for me and Dan." She smoothed down the fabric. "Olga told me there was danger for me at the circus." She gazed up at her sisters. "I didn't think she had a true gift, but maybe I was wrong."

"One thing," Phoebe pointed out. "There was no doubt that the guy with his paws around your throat was a serious looker. That doesn't sound at all like Prue's Mr. Ugly."

Piper looked at Prue. "Do you think the strange guy around Ivan's trailer could have something to do with Phoebe's vision?"

Prue sat down on the couch on the other side of Piper. "I don't know. When I saw Olga she was protecting herself from the evil eye that she thought she might catch from Ivan. Maybe this strange Gypsy has something to do with that."

"Time to check *The Book of Shadows*," Phoebe declared, rising to her feet. "We should see if there's anything on Gypsies in it. Maybe we'll find something on the decaying guy in the bushes."

"Of course, he could just be a weirdo creep. They have those hanging around circuses and parks, too," Piper reminded them. She shuddered. "Maybe you were right to be creeped out by the circus," she said to Prue.

"You two start," Prue said. "I need to get these proofs developed. I cut out early on the first day of an assignment. I should at least show up with some great prints tomorrow."

"We're on it," Phoebe said. She and Piper headed up to the attic, where they kept *The Book of Shadows*. The thick and beautiful book held many spells written down by previous generations of Halliwell witches. Phoebe felt certain they'd find some answers in it. She felt much better, now that she and her sisters were working on preventing her vision from coming true.

After about an hour, they still hadn't found anything. Phoebe stretched. "Let's quit for a bit," she suggested. "Come back fresh. I need a snack, and I'll bet Prue needs a break."

Piper rubbed her face and blinked a few times. "Okay. My eyes could use a rest. Some of the writing in this book is tiny."

They went downstairs to the darkroom Prue had set up in the basement. "Prue!" Phoebe called through the door. "Is it safe to come in?"

"Enter!" Prue said.

Piper and Phoebe stepped into the darkroom. Phoebe let her eyes adjust to the strange red glowing light. "How's it going?"

"Pretty good," Prue replied, swirling a pair of tongs in a tray filled with developing solution. "How's it going with your research?"

Piper sighed. "Let's just say we hope your pictures are developing better than the leads are."

Prue raised an eyebrow. "That good?"

"So can we see what you've got?" Phoebe asked.

"I'm finishing up the last roll, but there are some fun ones of you and those clowns," Prue said. "Over there, drying."

Piper and Phoebe examined the photos that Prue had already finished developing. "Some of these are really excellent," Phoebe said.

"I have to admit, the circus didn't turn out to be all that bad," Prue confessed.

"Gee. Could a handsome Gypsy have anything to do with that?" Piper teased. "Is he in here?" She waved at the drying photographs.

"He's on this last roll," Prue said, indicating the pictures in the tray in front of her. "I do have to say, after meeting Ivan, my opinion of people in the circus did change."

"What do you mean?" Phoebe asked.

"I never realized circus performers could be so down-to-earth," Prue explained.

"Because they spend time up on high wires and trapezes?" Phoebe asked.

"Why shouldn't they be normal people?" Piper demanded. "I'm surprised at you, Prue. You've been stereotyping circus performers all this time. Well, I'm glad that Ivan helped you see that."

"I guess he has," Prue said.

"Okay, enough chitchat about this miracle Gypsy man," Phoebe said. "What does the dude look like? All I could tell from where I was sitting was that he knew his way around a violin and has great legs."

Prue smiled at a photograph she was holding up. "These actually do him justice," she said. "Great." She plopped it into the rinsing tray and picked up another one.

"Let me see," Piper said. She squeezed in next to Prue and looked into the tray. "Not bad," she murmured appraisingly.

"My turn." Phoebe edged Piper away from the small table. She gasped.

She gripped the sides of the table to hold herself steady. She stared down into the tray, then up at her sisters.

"This guy in the photograph?" she said. She pointed down at him with a trembling finger. "This is the good-looking guy strangling Piper in my vision!"

CHAPTER 7

Prue gaped at Phoebe. "Wh-what are you talking about?"

"I'd recognize that handsome face anywhere," Phoebe insisted. "He's the guy with his fingers wrapped around Piper's throat."

Piper's hands flew up to her neck. "Are you sure?"

"There must be some kind of mistake," Prue protested. "Ivan doesn't seem capable of hurting anyone. I've seen him with his animals—"

"Maybe he feels differently about people," Phoebe commented.

"Or witches," added Piper.

Prue shook her head. "You haven't met him. I don't know how to explain it, but he is the gentlest person I've ever met."

"Demons and warlocks come in all guises," Phoebe reminded her. "One minute a guy is as sweet as mocha-chip ice cream. Then without any warning he's trying to zap a girl into oblivion."

Prue bit her lip. She knew that what Phoebe was saying was true, but it was hard to put together the Ivan that she had spent the afternoon with and the Ivan in Phoebe's vision.

"Let's not jump to any conclusions," Piper said. "You said that there are rumors that Ivan is cursed, right?"

Prue nodded.

"Well, maybe he really is," Piper continued, "and this curse will lead him to become violent or compel him to hurt me."

"Or maybe he's spreading the rumor himself," Phoebe countered. "It could be his alibi for any of his bad behavior."

Prue ran over all the facts she had and realized she didn't have very many. She had her gut instinct that Ivan didn't have a cruel bone in his body. But her experience as a witch told her that her feelings could sometimes be manipulated, or someone's true nature masked.

"What about that creepy Gypsy you saw near Ivan's trailer?" Phoebe said. "Could he have something to do with this?"

"I'm sure he does." Prue sighed. "But what?"

"Maybe it's part of the curse," Piper suggested. "Maybe it's the manifestation of the evil or something."

"Or maybe that gross guy is actually Ivan," Phoebe suggested darkly. "He was hanging around his trailer."

"Oh, it couldn't be," Prue blurted.

Phoebe gave Prue a stern look. "You don't know that."

Prue felt a pang. She knew Phoebe was right. She couldn't let her attraction to Ivan get in the way of clear thinking. If she allowed her feelings to cloud her judgment she could put them all in danger.

Including Ivan, she realized. Maybe there really was a curse, and it was up to the Charmed Ones to lift it. "This could be why you had the vision," she said to Phoebe. "Could Ivan be the innocent we're supposed to protect? Prevent him from doing this terrible thing against his will?"

"I think it's a lot more likely that my vision was a warning to Piper," Phoebe said.

"Obviously, we need more information," Prue said, rubbing the spot between her eyes. She felt a headache coming on. "We need to figure out who or what that creepy guy was. And to check out what's really up with Ivan and why he would attack Piper."

"We may not know why," Phoebe declared, "but we do know who. So at least we can keep Piper away from him."

"Phoebe's right," Prue said. "No more circus for you."

Piper sighed. "That won't work on two counts. A—if Ivan is a secret demon, we may need the Power of Three to defeat him."

"What's B?" Prue asked.

"Jenny begged me to take her back to the show while she's here visiting," Piper replied.

"Let me guess," Prue commented. "You felt so guilty about breaking up with Dan that you promised you'd take her."

"You can't!" Phoebe protested. "You were definitely on the losing side in the vision."

Piper crossed her arms over her chest. "Look. You don't even know where he's supposed to attack me. It may not be at the circus at all. And I am not breaking a promise to Jenny. We hauled her out of there before she really had any fun."

"Piper," Prue said.

"Prue," Piper said, mimicking Prue's warning tone. "I just won't do it," she insisted. "Jenny isn't all that thrilled to be here in the first place, and the first thing she hears when she arrives is that Dan and I broke up. I'm not going to add to that by going back on a promise."

Prue knew her sister well enough to know that there was no point in even trying to argue with her on the subject. To Piper a promise was golden.

"I will steer clear of Ivan," Piper said.

"And we'll try to make sure he steers clear of you," Phoebe said.

"I'll cover Ivan," Prue said.

"Are you sure that's a good idea?" Phoebe asked. "You seem a little, well, not exactly impartial on the subject."

"He might open up to me," Prue pointed out.

"Or he might open you up and eat your guts," Phoebe grumbled.

Prue gave her sister a disgusted look. "Eew. Did you have to go there? I will be careful." She let out a long sigh. "Just when I was beginning to actually enjoy the circus. This isn't the greatest way to get me to change my mind."

*   *   *

The next day Prue answered a knock at the door bright and early.

"Hi!" Jenny greeted her, a huge grin on her face. "Ready to go?"

Prue couldn't help but smile. Jenny was obviously really excited about going back to the carnival. Piper had been right. Jenny would have been very disappointed if they had canceled on her.

Prue's first official interview wasn't until somewhat later. She was going to use her cover as photographer to poke around. Piper and Phoebe were going to see what they could find out about other performers, including what they might know of Ivan. Phoebe was also going to try to have another vision.

"Did you get good tires?" Jenny asked as Prue drove them all back to the Carnival Cavalcade.

"Tires?" Prue repeated, confused.

Phoebe shot Prue a look. "Great tires," she said.

"Excellent tires," Piper chimed in.

"Good," Jenny declared. "So we can stay today as long as we want."

We'll stay as long as it takes, Prue thought, pulling into a parking space.

A few moments later, Prue hurried over to Ivan's trailer. She knocked on his door, feeling apprehensive as she waited for him to respond.

She shook her head. How can I figure out if he's evil without giving anything away? She just didn't believe he was a demon. The only vibes I get from him are sweet and kind, she thought.

And it's not because of his huge dark brown eyes and his mop of thick dark curls. Not a bit.

Get a grip, she ordered herself. Don't prove your sisters right—that you've lost all objectivity.

She knocked again harder. "Ivan?" she called.

He must not be inside, Prue told herself. She glanced around. Well, she decided, this looks like a perfect opportunity to do some snooping.

She concentrated on the lock, focused her energy, and with a sharp flick of her finger, opened the door.

She stepped into the trailer.

Every inch was crammed with costumes, souvenirs from places the circus had traveled, and family photos. In spite of the cheerful clutter, the trailer was neat and tidy.

Where should she start her search? She picked up a framed picture. A striking dark-haired couple smiled at the camera. A small mop-haired boy stood in front of them, holding a violin. The instrument was nearly as big as the boy. The child practically glowed, gazing at the violin with obvious awe. Prue had seen that same proud expression on Ivan's face when he talked about his family.

She replaced the photograph, and another picture caught her eye. An illustration was tacked to the door of the closet. Fingering it gently, Prue realized it had been torn from a book. The caption read "Gypsy in Traditional Costume." Beside it were sketches for costume ideas, with fabric swatches attached.

"Piper was right," Prue murmured. The clothes resembled those worn by the ghoulish figure she had seen yesterday.

Prue continued to search through Ivan's belongings, careful to replace any items she moved. So far nothing had indicated that Ivan was evil. Maybe I should bring Phoebe back here with me, she thought. Phoebe might be able to call up another vision with these objects, because I am striking out.

Prue crouched beside a large trunk. Using her powers, she flicked open the locks and popped open the top. All she found were extra costumes.

She stood and gave the room one last once-over. Her eyes widened as a shuddering wave of energy disrupted the air around the trunk.

"What the—"

Ivan's violin materialized right in front of her.

CHAPTER 8

Prue stood frozen, staring at the violin. Okay, something magical is definitely going on here, she thought. But what does it mean?

She took a step closer to the trunk. Was the violin itself magic, or had someone used magic on it?

Before she could investigate further, she heard the door open behind her. She scrunched her eyes shut. Uh-oh. Busted.

She whirled around and came face-to-face with Ivan. She was almost embarrassed by how much she liked looking at his face, despite the confusion that played across it right now.

"Prue, how did you get in?" he asked. "I thought I locked the door."

"It opened," Prue said. Which was the truth, in a way.

Ivan ran a hand through his curls. "I have to be more careful. Someone has taken my violin. Perhaps it was due to my own carelessness that they were able to get in."

"Someone took the violin?" Prue asked.

"Yes." He looked very upset. "That's where I've been. I was trying to find out who might have stolen it." He plopped down onto a chair beside the small table, his shoulders slumped. "I had hoped it was simply a curious child or a harmless prank. I would hate to think someone with the show would actually steal it."

"It's sitting right there." Prue pointed at the trunk. She carefully watched his reaction.

Ivan leaped to his feet. He picked up the violin gently and cradled it. "Where did you come from?" he asked the instrument.

"Are you expecting it to answer?" Prue asked.

Ivan laughed. A tiny blush crept across his cheeks. "Of course not," he stammered. "I—I feel very connected to the instrument. That is all."

"It is quite special," Prue said. "I mean, how many violins can vanish and then reappear all on their own?"

"That would make quite a circus act," Ivan joked. "Perhaps I should suggest it to Mr. Amalfi."

"So what do you think happened?" Prue asked.

Ivan shook his head. "Perhaps I never lost it at all. I've been terribly distracted lately. I could have put it somewhere and then forgot."

"It would be pretty tough to miss, sitting on top of the trunk," Prue pointed out.

"Yes, yes. But I have a good deal on my mind."

"About the violin?"

"I have misplaced it several times since the start of the show. It is terribly unlike me."

"What has you so distracted?" Prue pressed on.

"Some personal problems. Also some bad luck seems to be following me. Missed cues, sprung locks on the cages."

"Has all the bad luck involved the act?"

"Yes." He laughed. "I'll tell you something silly. Olga the fortune-teller actually tried to convince me that the violin itself was causing the bad luck. That it has a curse on it."

Prue wondered if the fortune-teller was right. So far Olga was batting a thousand. She had already predicted danger for Piper, a prediction confirmed by Phoebe's vision.

"Do you think maybe Olga has a point?" Prue asked.

Ivan's eyebrows raised. "Don't tell me you believe in such nonsense." He gave Prue a warm grin. "Here I am, the Gypsy, telling the gaujo not to be so superstitious. Ironic, yes?"

Not if you knew who I really am, Prue thought. "I believe there are things that are difficult to explain."

Ivan gave a dismissive wave of his hand. "This is simply a beautiful instrument, its magic is only the magic of its original craftsman." Ivan held up the violin and admired it. "I have lived with this violin all of my life, and I never tire of it."

He picked up a bow and played a quick melody. The notes sent tingles of delight through Prue. How could I ever have doubted him? she wondered. Instead of being worried that she might be in danger *from* him, she was worried *for* him.

She watched as he closed his eyes and swayed with the melody. His fingers moved along the violin's neck and the bow gracefully arced back and forth.

The bow. Prue saw that the narrow bow was intricately carved. She hadn't noticed that before. When Ivan had finished the tune, he spun the violin around and she caught sight of painted symbols covering the back of the violin. She guessed she had been so focused on Ivan that she hadn't paid that much attention to the violin—until it did a little circus act all on its own.

"Why would Olga tell you the violin was cursed?" Prue asked. She wondered if those symbols spelled evil in Romany, the Gypsy language.

"Probably so she could then have me pay her a lot of money to remove the so-called curse." Ivan shrugged. "It's a classic scam. Tell some gullible believer that they have a terrible curse on their head and that for a thousand dollars the shuvani will take the curse off."

"*Shuvani?*" Piper repeated.

"It's the Gypsy word for 'witch' or 'wise woman,' " Ivan explained.

"You believe that Olga was trying to pull a scam on you? Another Gypsy?" Prue asked.

"Up until that day, I had never spoken a word to Olga. Neither one of us would know for certain if the 'Gypsy' attached to our names was real or not. Many people in the circus invent exotic backgrounds. It adds to the mystique. It was perfectly possible that she thought I was just another gaujo—until I spoke Rom to her."

"But she persisted?" Prue asked. "Why would she do that unless she truly believed it was cursed."

Ivan rubbed his face. Prue wondered if she was pushing him too far. She couldn't stop now though—she had to get to the bottom of this. Her sister's life was at stake. And so, quite possibly, was Ivan's.

Finally, he said, "This is a very valuable instrument. Worth hundreds of thousands of dollars. Why wouldn't she want it? But I don't like thinking that of another performer."

"Ivan?" A woman with auburn hair popped her head into the trailer doorway.

"Miranda, come in." Ivan stood.

Miranda frowned when she saw Prue. She stepped inside and crossed to Ivan. Standing beside him, she glared at Prue. "Who is this?"

"I'm Prue Halliwell," Prue said. "I'm working for 415 magazine. I'm the photographer."

The woman nodded. She was seriously frosty. Her high cheekbones and sharp straight nose gave her a haughty appearance. It didn't help that her bright green eyes were sending icicles in Prue's direction.

"This lovely lady is Miranda Merrill, the tightrope walker," Ivan said. "Her family is well-known throughout Europe."

"That's really interesting," Prue said, hoping to warm things up. "Be sure to tell that to Kristin, the journalist. I know she plans to interview you."

Miranda turned her back on Prue and began to study her appearance in the mirror. "I haven't decided if I will agree to be interviewed. I don't think outsiders should be allowed such open access." She sent Prue a withering look in the mirror, then turned and addressed Ivan. "You shouldn't be wasting your time talking to her. What would she know of your life? Our life?"

Way to be hostile, Miranda, Prue thought. "Perhaps the article can present the life as you would like it to be known," Prue suggested.

Miranda focused her large green eyes on Prue again. She gave Prue a condescending once over. "I don't think reporters can truly be trusted."

Prue had the feeling that Miranda simply didn't trust anyone anywhere near Ivan, reporters or not. She wondered if Miranda was the personal issue that Ivan had found distracting. Well, hanging around Ivan wasn't going to make Miranda warm up to her any. It wouldn't be a good idea for her to alienate Miranda so badly that she refused to be interviewed or photographed.

"I hope we will see each other later," Prue said to Miranda. "Bye, Ivan."

Prue stepped out of the trailer. As soon as the door closed she heard an argument begin. She couldn't make out the words, but she could hear that the voices were raised and the tone was angry. Not wanting to eavesdrop, Prue hurried away.

Her questions about Ivan's personal life could wait. Prue had a more urgent problem. How can I get a better look at those symbols? Prue wondered. She felt that they were the key to the mystery behind the violin.

Her head snapped up. "That's it," she murmured. Trusty telephoto lens. During the performance, I'll shoot with the telephoto from angles that will catch the markings. We might actually solve the mystery of that instrument after all.

*   *   *

Phoebe leaned against the back of a spin-art booth. Cautiously, she crept to the edge and peered around the side. She let out a deep sigh. Coast was clear.

Just my luck, she thought. I'm invisible to the cute riggers and I'm irresistible to Raphael the Tattooed Snake Charmer. What is up with that?

She had wasted most of the morning playing hide-and-please-don't-seek with Ralphie-boy. He was certainly persistent.

She really wanted to check out the area in the woods where Prue had seen the creepy tattered Gypsy. She hoped to find something the person had dropped, or maybe discover some vagrant living out there. Something to give them a clue to go on. But she wasn't completely certain where the animal cages were, and she sure didn't want to ask Ivan. So who could she ask without drawing suspicion?

"Is that my darling Phoebe?" a rough voice called out behind her. "Wait up, girlie!"

Every muscle in Phoebe's body tensed: Raphael. She broke into a sprint—and charged right into a juggling stilt walker.

"Hey!" the stilt walker cried. Beanbags flew everywhere and kids started laughing. The stilt walker desperately tried to regain his balance. No such luck. He tumbled down onto Phoebe.

"I'm really, really sorry." Phoebe scrambled to her feet, trying to drag the guy up with her, but because his legs were attached to stilts the operation was hugely awkward.

"Sorry, but I've really really got to get out of here!" Normally she'd stick around and help the poor white-faced performer gather the beanbags and get up, but Raphael was closing in fast. She dashed away, and the stilt walker tumbled back to the ground.

"You're lucky I wasn't juggling clubs," he shouted angrily after her.

Another person I'm going to have to avoid at this carnival, Phoebe noted. First the snake guy, now the stilt walker.

"Phoebeeeeee!" Raphael crooned. "Slow down. I'm not as spry as I used to be!"

That's a bit of luck for me for a change! Phoebe put on speed. She dashed in and out of the booths along the midway, concentrating on avoiding knocking anyone over or slamming into anything. Within a few minutes she was near a cluster of trailers.

She glanced around. Raphael was nowhere in sight. I know what I'll do, she decided. I'll knock on a few doors to see if I can get some background dirt on Ivan.

A small boy, about five years old, wearing sweatpants and a Carnival Cavalcade T-shirt stared at Phoebe.

"Hey, cutie," Phoebe said. She knelt down to speak to him face-to-face.

The boy's eyes widened. He backed up a few steps, then turned and darted away between the trailers.

"That was strange," Phoebe muttered, standing back up. "Am I truly that repellent?"

Phoebe heard a door bang open. Three clowns in full makeup came around the side of a trailer where the boy had vanished. They wore the same striped orange-and-yellow full-body leotards and oversize hats. It was impossible to tell them apart.

"Hiya!" Phoebe said brightly. She didn't recognize these three clowns. Even with the makeup she could tell they weren't Masha, Sacha, or Kaboodle. "I'm Phoebe. I was wondering if I could ask you a few questions?"

"No one is allowed in Clown Alley but clowns," clown number one said.

"Clown Alley?" Phoebe wasn't sure why these guys were so hostile, but it was pretty obvious that the little boy had ratted on her and they viewed her as a trespasser.

Clown number two put his hands on his hips. "Clown Alley. Our turf. Now vamoose."

"But—" Phoebe sputtered.

"Come along," clown number three said. He took her arm and turned her around. One of the other clowns gripped her other arm.

"Hey!" The two guys had her in a firm grip. They led her back to the barricades separating the trailer camp from the midway.

"Fine, be that way," Phoebe huffed.

"Don't come back," one guy warned.

"Don't worry, I won't," Phoebe retorted. "You know," she called after them, "for guys who make their living by being funny, you don't have much sense of humor."

They slipped behind a trailer. Sheesh. Maybe Prue had the right idea about clowns after all.

Phoebe put her hands on her hips. Now what?

"Please, please, please," Jenny whined.

Piper blew her bangs away from her face. Jenny

was being particularly difficult today. All the girl wanted to do was try to find Ivan—which was definitely not on Piper's to-do list. In fact, it topped the to-don't! The only other idea Jenny had was to return to Olga's vardo.

"I have a special magic request," Jenny explained. "It's really important."

Piper had hoped to avoid Olga for two reasons. If Olga truly did have second sight, Piper didn't want her to identify her as a witch. She was also afraid Olga might actually be successful in casting Jenny's spell. And Piper had the sinking feeling that the magic Jenny wanted Olga to perform was a love spell reuniting Piper and Dan.

Still, she couldn't figure out any way to talk Jenny out of visiting Olga. Since Piper had nixed the Ivan meeting, she felt she needed to humor the girl with something. Deciding between an encounter with Olga or an encounter with Ivan, Piper knew which way she had to go.

"Olga it is," Piper declared.

Jenny and Piper wove through the crowds to Olga's colorful vardo. Olga was sitting out front at the card table, fanning herself with a set of cards. Her thick dark eyebrow raised as she watched Jenny and Piper approach. She obviously remembers us, Piper observed. Or at least me.

"Hi." Jenny beamed.

"Hello," Olga replied. "Have you come to consult the cards again?"

"No," Jenny said. "Something much more important." She gave Piper a guick sidelong glance. A slight blush tinted her cheeks as she thrust a hand into her purse. She pulled out a fistful of ribbons. "Will you show me how to tie magic love knots?"

"You know the love secrets of the Gypsies?" Olga asked.

"I've heard about them," Jenny said. "Do they really work?"

Olga nodded. "I have known many a happy union bound by just such bindings," she replied.

I really wish Olga wouldn't encourage Jenny, Piper thought. We could wind up in serious trouble.

"Ooh, I wish I had the Romany ruby," Jenny exclaimed. "Then my love spell would be three times as powerful!"

Olga dropped the cards she'd been holding. There was no mistaking her startled expression.

"How do you speak of such things?" the woman demanded in a harsh whisper.

"Is the Romany ruby a secret?" Jenny asked. She glanced at Piper, obviously worried that she had said something wrong.

"It is known only to the Gypsies," Olga said. "How do you come by such knowledge?" She eyed Piper suspiciously. Piper had the distinct impression that Olga believed Piper had figured out the gypsy lore through her own witch power. That could prove problematic.

"Ivan told my sister about Gypsy folklore," Piper explained. She wanted to give Olga the impression that she didn't believe in the Romany ruby. "And my sister told us. I've told Jenny she shouldn't believe such nonsense."

"You did not!" Jenny protested.

"Who is your sister?" Olga asked. "Is she with the carnival?"

"Oh, no," Piper said. "Prue's a photographer, and she's here doing a story about the carnival. We just tagged along."

That reminded her that she should see if Phoebe had come up with anything. "In fact, we should get going. Phoebe will probably be looking for us."

"I thought you said her name was Prue," Olga asked, puzzled.

"That's my other sister," Piper explained.

"There are three of them," Jenny said. "I'll bet that's lucky, isn't it?"

Something about Olga's smile looked false to Piper. Of course, that could be because she was still disturbed that Ivan had revealed some Gypsy secrets to outsiders.

"Three is always lucky," Olga said to Jenny. Then she locked eyes with Piper. "But why don't you heed my warnings? Have I not told you there is danger here? Stay away from Ivan. He has a dark sign upon him and will bring only harm to those near him."

CHAPTER
9

Jenny turned saucer-size eyes on Piper. "We have to warn Prue!" she exclaimed. She turned back to Olga. "Piper's sister has a big crush on Ivan," she explained.

Piper was pretty certain Prue wouldn't want her personal life broadcast at the circus. "Prue can take care of herself," Piper assured Jenny.

Then a thought occurred to her. What if Ivan strangled her because she was trying to save Prue from him? Were any of them safe at the circus?

She decided to question Olga. She wasn't sure if Olga was truly magical or simply a good actress and con artist. But she might have information about Ivan. And if she really was a shuvani—Gypsy witch—then her powers might be just the thing they needed to vanquish Ivan. On the other hand, Olga seemed to be afraid of the handsome violinist. She might not want to get involved. Then Piper would have blown her cover for nothing.

She at least had to pump Olga for info. Only how could she do that with Jenny there?

Before Piper could figure out what to do, a trio of giggling teenage girls burst in. "We want our fortunes told," a tall redhead demanded.

"I don't," a spiky-haired girl declared. "I want to hear yours."

"Olga will take care of you all," the fortune-teller said. "First we must clear the room and the energy fields."

I can take a hint, Piper thought. That's our cue to leave.

"Thanks for everything," Piper said.

"But we didn't get the love knots," Jenny complained.

"I don't think we need any of those," Piper said.

"Are we going to warn Prue about Ivan?" Jenny asked.

"I—I don't think that's really necessary," Piper replied. "I think Olga has a vivid imagination." She didn't want Jenny asking too many questions about occult goings-on. The subject hit too close to home.

"So what are we going to do now?" Jenny asked.

"Find Phoebe and go to the performance in the tent," Piper said.

They wandered the midway looking for Phoebe. Piper hoped Phoebe was having better luck getting information than she'd had.

Jenny had perked up, Piper was pleased to notice. She must have given up on the idea that the carnival was for babies. Without having to prove that she was a sophisticated lady to her uncle Dan, Jenny could relax into being the fun-loving twelve-year-old she actually was. Jenny played every single game along the midway, and then they ate almost every junk food snack that was offered for sale. Jenny was oblivious to the sense of danger lurking just on the outskirts. All the time, though, Piper couldn't shake the creepy feeling that they were being watched. Were Piper's fears real or imagined? Hard to say, but in her experience she had learned to trust her demon radar.

"Missy!" someone called. Piper turned around and came face-to-face with Raphael. Luckily he was minus his snake. His bad breath and sweaty body odor hadn't disappeared, however.

"I was trying to place you and your young friend," Raphael said, gesturing to Jenny, who was at a nearby booth. She was shooting a stream of water into a fish bowl, trying to win a prize. "Then I remembered! You were with my dear Phoebe yesterday."

Could Raphael have been the person following us? Piper wondered. That would be a relief, since she had a feeling his only interest in the Halliwells was limited to her younger sister. His intentions toward her may not be exactly angelic, but they certainly wouldn't qualify as demonic.

"That's right," Piper replied. "She's my sister."

"I should have known. Good looks run in families." He flashed a grin at her.

Doesn't the circus have a dental plan? Piper wondered, trying not to stare at his gold tooth. He could sure use it.

Jenny finished her game and joined Piper and Raphael. "Look what I won!" She held up a stuffed purple fish.

"Good for you!" Piper said.

"I was just saying to your friend here," Raphael told Jenny, "that I've been looking for that lovely Phoebe, but she seems to have given me the slip."

Piper bit her lip. I'm not surprised, she thought.

"We were looking for her, too," Jenny said. "We haven't seen her anywhere."

"We'll tell her you're looking for her," Piper added. "Right now, though, we have to be somewhere." She didn't want Raphael to try to tag along.

"Good luck," Jenny called. She and Piper hurried away from Raphael along the midway.

Jenny started giggling. "He's pretty gross, isn't he? But he seems nice."

"But definitely not Phoebe's type," Piper said.

"Definitely not," Jenny agreed. "I wonder whose type he would be?"

Piper shook her head. "I'm not sure." She grinned. "His snake, Isabella, seems very fond of him."

Phoebe darted out from between a lemonade stand and a guess-your-weight booth. "There you are," she said. She gave a quick glance around. "Ralphie-boy isn't here, is he?"

"No, we left him back by the fish fight booth," Piper reported.

"Good. Uh, Jenny, would you mind getting me some caramel popcorn? I have a total craving. I saw a stand a few booths back."

"Sure! Can I have some, too?"

"Of course, my treat," Phoebe said. She handed Jenny some bills and pointed out the booth. It had a long line in front of it.

"Be back in a minute. Want any, Piper?" she asked.

Piper patted her stomach. "One more bite of junk food and I think my teeth will crack and my stomach will explode."

"Okay." Jenny dashed to the booth and stood in line.

"I'll make this quick," Phoebe said, her voice low. "I don't want Jenny to overhear."

"You found out something?"

"Not exactly. But I think I know how to get some information. I have a plan. Meet me at Ivan's trailer at exactly seven forty-five. Only make sure no one notices you."

"What do I do with Jenny?" Piper asked. "She's my responsibility."

Phoebe's brow crinkled. "I don't know. Think of something."

Piper noticed Phoebe's eyes focus on something just beyond her. Her face registered dismay. "Uh-oh," Phoebe said. "Raphael sighting at ten o'clock. Gotta go. Now, don't forget. Lose Jenny. And be there!"

Piper watched Phoebe race away. She dashed up to Jenny, who had finally made it to the front of the line. Piper watched as Jenny purchased the caramel popcorn and handed one box to Phoebe. Then Phoebe took off at a quick clip.

"Was that Phoebe?" Raphael asked as he jogged up to Piper. "Ah, well. Just my luck. You'd think Ivan's curse had rubbed off on me. I'm having no luck with women."

"Is Ivan's curse about women?" Piper asked.

"What?" Raphael asked, confused. "Oh, no, no. He's just been having a run of bad luck. Although I believe he's unlucky in love right now. Make that, his lady friend is the one who is unlucky."

Before Piper could ask anything else, Jenny returned. She offered the caramel popcorn to Piper and Raphael, who both turned it down.

"So should we head for the tent?" Jenny asked.

Piper checked her watch. "Sure. We're early, but there's always a clown show before it begins."

They walked to the tent. The whole time Piper wondered how she could slip away from Jenny and what Phoebe's plan might be.

Phoebe checked her watch again. It was 7:40:12—which made it twelve seconds later than the last time she'd checked her watch.

Phoebe hoped that Ivan really was as habitual as his fellow performers had claimed. While Phoebe was dodging Raphael, she had managed to ask the performers living in the trailers near Ivan a few questions. What each of them told her was that Ivan left for the first of the evening performances at precisely 7:50. Not a minute sooner, not a minute later. You could set a clock by him, Giorgio the acrobat had told her. His trailer was right next door, so he should know.

Phoebe peered out of her hiding place in the bushes beside Ivan's trailer. Is this a mistake? she wondered. Maybe I shouldn't be bringing Piper into his clutches. Could I actually be making the vision come true?

Not possible, Phoebe reminded herself. Ivan will be off to the tent, safely onstage. If worse comes to worst, Piper can freeze him. And if he doesn't freeze, well, that would put Piper in danger, but it certainly would be proof that he isn't human.

Stay calm, Phoebe ordered herself. It's not going to play that way. He'll be out of the trailer and occupied at the tent. It will work out fine.

She spotted a figure sneaking toward her along the bushes: Piper. Phoebe popped up and waved her over. Piper crawled into the bushes beside her.

"Did you have trouble getting away from Jenny?" Phoebe whispered.

Piper shook her head. "The clowns were doing shtick and I told her I had to find a bathroom. I made her vow to stay put—which I knew wouldn't be a problem since she was deeply mesmerized by the performance."

"That's good. And she should be perfectly fine surrounded by the audience. It's not as if she's walking around by herself."

"I hope." Piper frowned. "I'm not very comfortable with this. How long will your plan take?"

Phoebe shook her head. "Don't know. How long do you think you can stay gone before Jenny comes looking for you?"

"Well, I don't know if anything would tear her away—particularly once Ivan starts performing. Besides, I told her I was going to search for a real bathroom instead of those port-o-potties. She agrees that they're gross, so it seemed a legit excuse."

Phoebe nodded. "Good one."

"So are you going to tell me the plan or are you going to make me guess?"

"Here goes." Phoebe explained about Ivan's obsessive punctuality. "The moment Ivan steps out of the trailer you freeze time just long enough for me to sneak inside. Once I'm in, unfreeze him. He'll lock the door and go on his merry way."

"And what will this accomplish?" Piper asked. "Prue already searched the trailer and came up empty."

"I'm really hoping that by handling Ivan's belongings I can have a vision," Phoebe explained. "A more helpful one. Or at least get a better idea of what is going on with him."

"Makes sense," Piper said.

"Okay, but you have to promise to keep out of Ivan's sight," Phoebe ordered. "I don't want you to risk making my vision come true."

"Deal," Piper agreed.

Phoebe was surprised that her sister didn't object to the breaking-and-entering portion of this plan. Usually Piper was strict about not using their magic in ways that might be frowned upon from a legal perspective. Then again, it was Piper being strangled in the vision. That future was something her sister would really like to cancel out. Phoebe figured Piper was as eager as she—no, make that *more* eager—to get to the bottom of this little supernatural mystery.

"There he is," Phoebe whispered. She glanced at her watch. The time was 7:45:00 exactly.

Piper gestured at Ivan, freezing him midstep.

"Well, at least we know he's human," Piper commented.

"You didn't leave me much room to slip by him," Phoebe complained.

"Good thing you're so fit and trim," Piper replied. "Go. Get. I need to get back to Jenny."

"Okie-dokie. But stay hidden."

"Of course. Now, scoot."

Phoebe crossed her fingers. "Send me visions luck," she said.

Piper crossed her fingers, then said, "Go. Before he unfreezes all on his own."

Phoebe clambered out of the bushes and raced toward Ivan's trailer. "Keep your paws off Piper," she snarled at the frozen man. She squeezed past him. "Hmm. Really glad I didn't have that second helping of fries at lunch," she commented. Then she waved at Piper and stepped into the trailer. Peering through a window, she watched Ivan suddenly come back to life.

She ducked below the window so she wouldn't risk being seen. Just in case he glanced back, Phoebe stepped into the tiny bathroom and behind the shower curtain. She didn't want him to see a shadow or movement of any kind.

She counted to one hundred before reaching for the shower curtain. She froze.

She heard the extremely recognizable sound of a key being turned in the lock!

CHAPTER
10

Phoebe froze in the shower. Luckily, she was able to squeeze behind the shower curtain completely.

Please don't come into the bathroom, she thought. Was there some kind of don't-come-in-here spell? She decided not to risk trying to create one. If it didn't work, even a whispered chant would probably grab Ivan's attention and lead him straight to her.

Phoebe frantically tried to come up with possible excuses if Ivan came in, but since she couldn't think of a single one, she just crossed her fingers for luck and hoped for the best.

She listened intently. She could hear that he was coming closer . . . closer . . .

Oh, no! He'd walked right into the bathroom! She could hear the medicine cabinet swing open. She shut her eyes. I can't catch a break tonight! Uh-oh. If I hope he doesn't decide to shower, that's probably exactly what he'll do. Things just seem to be going against me.

Phoebe tried to breathe as silently as she could. She dared not ruffle the shower curtain with any stray movement or even the slightest current of air. She knew the medicine cabinet reflected her hiding place. Ivan would be sure to notice.

She could hear Ivan brushing his teeth. No wonder he has such pearly whites—he probably flosses, too! Why did he have to have such good dental hygiene? Finally, he rinsed and spit. Even a guy as handsome as Ivan couldn't make spitting sound like anything but spitting, Phoebe observed. Then, to Phoebe's great relief, Ivan left the trailer one more time.

I really hope he's done for a while. This was something of a departure from his ordinary schedule, she realized. Maybe the bad luck mojo is rattling his nerves and throwing off his routine.

Once she felt sure Ivan wouldn't be back, Phoebe climbed out of the shower. She picked up his toothbrush since that had been the most recent object her subject had touched.

Nothing.

Phoebe stepped out of the bathroom and glanced around. What would be the most likely object to trigger a vision? She was still working on calling up the visions by her own will. She ran her fingers through scarves dangling from a clothing hook. She even lay on Ivan's bed, spreading her arms wide. She knelt on the bed and held the pillow on her lap.

Nothing.

Now Phoebe began to pace. She wasn't sure how

long she should risk being in Ivan's trailer. What if someone noticed her moving around inside? Luckily Ivan had left a few lights on so she wasn't stumbling around in the dark. But her silhouette might be visible from outside. She needed to hurry.

Photographs—nothing. Books—nothing. Shoes—nothing. Nothing nothing nothing!

This is so frustrating! Phoebe snatched up a hairbrush from the dresser and smacked it against her hands.

She was immediately engulfed in flames.

The heat was unbearable. Red-and-golden flames licked all around her, singeing her flesh. She could practically smell her hair burning. In horror, she threw up her hands and crumpled to the floor. The hairbrush clattered a few feet away.

These branches sure are scratchy, Piper thought. She sat in the bushes, staring at Ivan's trailer, wondering what Phoebe might find.

It seemed pretty unlikely that Prue would have a crush on a demon. That seems to be more my territory, Piper thought ruefully. I'm the one with the lousy track record.

Not that her track record was much better with nondemons. The whole Dan and Leo situation wasn't her most shining hour. She had truly done the best she could to spare everyone's feelings, and of course everyone had suffered—at least a little bit, anyway.

Even Jenny was affected by our breakup, Piper thought. I hadn't added that into the equation of disappointment. Well, there was nothing she could do about that. Pleasing twelve-year-olds isn't exactly a reason to have a relationship.

Piper shifted restlessly. She didn't like leaving Jenny alone for very long. The girl was her responsibility, and there might be a demon running around. She knew Jenny wouldn't budge from her seat—she'd be too riveted by the show. She should be perfectly safe sitting in the audience. Still . . .

But Piper also couldn't leave Phoebe without a lookout. Of course, they had neglected to come up with any kind of signal to let Phoebe know if anyone was coming. Well, Piper would have to freeze them, dash in and grab Phoebe, and then book it out of there.

Peering from her hiding place, Piper watched several performers heading over to the performance tent. Kaboodle and Masha were holding hands like teenagers.

"Come along, dearies," a shrill voice called out. A plump woman wearing several colorful petticoats and a tight corsetlike top minced along the path. She was followed by five small dogs wearing identical skirts. Piper recognized the woman from the show the previous night: Mitzi and her Performing Poodles.

Uh-oh. One of the poodles broke ranks. It headed straight for Piper. The little critter snuffled around the bush, right near her toes. I shouldn't have worn these sandals, Piper scolded herself. If that little dog starts licking my bare feet, I'm not going to be able to control myself. I'm going to start giggling.

"Snookums," Mitzi called. "What are you doing? We have to get to the tent."

Snookums continued pawing at the bush near Piper. Oh, great. Now the flouncy petticoat was caught on one of the branches. The dog started tugging and yipping, trying to get free.

"Ooh, Snookums, don't tear your dress!" Mitzi hurried over to help her poodle. Piper was about to throw her hands up to freeze Mitzi before she discovered her, but she just didn't move fast enough. That will teach me to debate a freeze, she scolded herself. Next time, just go for it.

Mitzi's eyes widened as she stared straight into Piper's face. "What are you doing hiding in the bushes?" she demanded.

"Uh, uh, I . . ." Piper tried to think of an excuse. She didn't exactly want to say she was playing lookout for Phoebe.

Mitzi burst out laughing. She bent down and untangled her dog's dress and stood back up, cradling the poodle like a baby. "Of course. Another Ivan groupie."

"What?" Piper stared at Mitzi.

Snookums licked Mitzi's double chins. "I hate to tell you, dearie, but Ivan doesn't go for girls who throw themselves at him. And just between you and me, you'd better not let Miranda catch you out here. Come on, now, get up."

Piper scrambled out from the bushes. "Miranda?" she repeated.

"That Miranda," Mitzi confided. "She can be a real demon when she's jealous. She'd make mincemeat of a groupie like you."

Piper blushed. She hated having Mitzi think she was going to throw herself at Ivan. But it was better than having her know the real reason she was skulking in the bushes—that she was a snoopy witch!

"Now, run along," Mitzi admonished Piper. She took a wide stance between Piper and Ivan's trailer. She was obviously determined to wait until she was sure that Piper had gone before she'd move from that spot.

"Okay," Piper said reluctantly. There didn't seem anything else she could do but leave Phoebe alone in Ivan's trailer.

"Vamoose!" Mitzi ordered. "Do you want me to set my dogs on you?"

Piper stifled a laugh as she gazed at the poodles in petticoats. They didn't look like they were a match for even a kitten, but she got the point.

"I'm going," Piper said. She spun on her heel and took off down the path toward the tent. Well, she should check back in with Jenny anyway. Phoebe doesn't need my freezing ability to get out of the trailer, at least. She glanced down at her watch: 8:05. Ivan was backstage preparing to perform right now, Piper assured herself. Phoebe should be fine.

Phoebe lay on the floor of Ivan's trailer, gasping for breath. She coughed a few times. That was some vision, Phoebe thought. It was almost as if it was really happening to me—as if maybe this was a vision for myself.

Phoebe shuddered. What a horrifying thought.

She slowly got into a sitting position and leaned against Ivan's bed. Maybe the visions she consciously called up were more powerful. That was something she was still learning about.

Okay, what does the vision tell me? she asked herself. Not really much of anything, she realized. Because of the flames and the intensity, she didn't see anyone's face. She rose to her feet, waiting for the lightheadedness to disappear. Oh, man, how long was I out? she wondered. Her heart fluttered in panic—what if she'd been lying on the floor for Ivan's entire act?

She checked her watch and relief flooded through her. Only 8:10. She still had plenty of time. But she didn't want to push it. For one thing, she didn't think she could take another vision right away.

She turned toward the door. Her eyes widened. The knob was moving.

The door was flung open—and in walked Ivan!

CHAPTER
11

What are you doing in here?" Ivan demanded. Phoebe could see the suspicion and fury in his eyes.

"Aren't you supposed to be onstage now?" Phoebe demanded right back. She figured the best defense was a good offense.

So it doesn't always work.

"I'm on last, remember?" he answered, his eyes narrowing. "Now answer my question. What are you doing in my trailer?"

"Well, uh, the door opened up and I was looking for my sister," Phoebe said. Sheesh. Even I don't believe that line. Work harder at sounding confident, she scolded herself.

"Who's your sister?" He crossed his arms over his chest. "Why would she be in my trailer?"

"Prue Halliwell," Phoebe said. "The photographer for *415*?"

His expression never changed. Hmm. If Ivan was

as into Prue as Prue was into him, he should at least have warmed up a little at hearing Prue's name. There should be something the teensiest bit friendlier flickering in those big brown eyes.

Well, using Prue's name isn't helping, Phoebe realized. Better try a new approach.

"I'm a big fan," Phoebe cooed. Flattery usually worked with men.

Not this man. His face stayed hard, his eyes cold. "Just get out. I'm in a hurry. I have a performance, remember? I don't have time to deal with you."

"Fine, I'm going." She crossed to the door.

"Nothing better be missing," he shouted as he slammed the door behind her.

What does Prue see in this guy? Phoebe wondered. Sure, the features are technically handsome, but there's nothing warm or sexy about him. All that seemed to be in his face was cruelty and anger. He reeked of mean. This is the dude that has Prue going gaga? I really don't get it.

I can easily picture him as the man in my vision strangling Piper, she thought. In fact, I'm lucky he didn't rewrite the vision and strangle *me* right now. Where is the sweet gentle soul that has Prue so captivated? There is no charm to that man at all!

Phoebe stopped short. "That's it," she murmured. Ivan has Prue under a spell. Maybe he slipped her a love charm or potion.

She picked up her pace. We need to consult *The Book of Shadows* again. He's a Gypsy, so the most likely scenario is that it's a Gypsy spell. I wonder if there's a section in the book for magical traditions other than our own? Ooh, I really hope there's something on Gypsy magic in it. Piper's life—and maybe even Prue's—could depend on it.

Prue paced backstage, trying to ignore Kristin's nonstop chatter. Not only was Prue putting up with Kristin's never-ending monologue, she had spent the entire day photographing clowns. They seemed to be the performers Kristin liked best.

"I think it's so interesting that none of the clowns would allow us to photograph them without their makeup," Kristin said. "Although from what I understand, that's pretty common. I did some research, and there have been some clowns who wouldn't even let other circus folks see them in their natural faces." Kristin giggled. "Actually, I can relate. I never let anyone see me without *my* makeup!"

"Uh-huh," Prue murmured. She ran her fingers along her telephoto lens. She was trying to figure out her best chance of getting a clear shot of the back of Ivan's violin. She had managed to take some pictures of the carved bow in the dressing room as he prepared. But with magic, as Prue knew only too well, partial information could land you in terrible danger. She needed the whole story, or things could go horribly wrong. Prue might be able to find the intricate carvings on the bow in *The Book of Shadows*, but without the symbols on the back of the violin, their meaning wouldn't be accurate. Every element of a magical system worked together, so you had to untangle it piece by piece. In spell casting, changing a single element could dramatically alter the outcome of the spell. She figured the symbols on the back of the violin referenced or affected the carvings on the bow. She needed it all.

"Look at that," Kristin commented. Prue's eyes flicked to the ring. The clowns were chasing one another around the ring. Prue wasn't sure what Kristin was pointing out.

"The act is different tonight," Kristin commented. "Instead of six clowns, there are only five. I wonder why." She studied the performance a moment longer, then began scribbling. "Oooh! That's a good question. Do they change the act a bit each night to keep it fresh? Or was someone injured? How do they make the adjustments? How much of the act is improvisational?"

This was a tic of Kristin's that drove Prue nuts. She'd fire these questions at Prue as if Prue was supposed to have the answers. It had taken Prue the full two days they'd spent together so far to stop feeling put on the spot, or racking her brains for an answer. Finally, she figured out that all she needed to do was nod.

Besides, all these questions—as if discovering the secret of the clowns' performance was the key to world peace or something. She had enjoyed spending time with Kaboodle and Masha, she admitted. They were smart and sweet. But the rest of the clowns were just a putty-nosed blur. There were so many of them! And most of them seemed to think once they had their faces on, the performance began, in the ring or out. They just never quit, well, *clowning* around. What made that silly clown think spritzing her with water this afternoon was funny? In fact, why would *anyone* think that kind of humor was funny?

As she watched the clowns go through their paces, Prue noted that their act seemed to last longer than usual. Or was it that she just found it more tedious? No, she thought, glancing down at her watch, it is running longer.

Prue had learned that the clowns served more than one purpose in the show. Not only did they entertain the audience, but they often were used to cover up glitches—a reluctant animal, for example, a prop or a set problem, or any kind of delay backstage. Perhaps the reason the act was long tonight was a practical one. She wondered if Ivan could be the reason for the extended performance. He was scheduled next.

She glanced up into the stands and was relieved to see Piper in her seat. One more day that Phoebe's vision hadn't come true. Of course, the night isn't over yet, Prue reminded herself. She tapped her telephoto lens again. She was determined to get to the bottom of this. She had to keep her sister safe. And she wanted to discover the truth about Ivan. She simply couldn't believe Phoebe was right. But to prove her youngest sister wrong, Prue needed solid evidence.

"Excuse me," a haughty voice said. Prue turned to see who had the frosty tone.

Miranda Merrill, the tightrope walker, stalked past Prue, glaring as she went. "It is terribly dangerous for outsiders to be backstage," Miranda snapped. "Stay out of the way."

"I'm sorry," Prue said, giving the woman a wide berth.

"I don't know what Mr. Amalfi was thinking,"

Miranda muttered. She stood and placed herself at the edge of the ring. She was obviously there to watch Ivan's act. Or keep an eye on him.

Prue darted a glance at Miranda. The woman was truly breathtaking up on the high wire. She had a ballerina's grace and regal bearing. She was obviously very skilled at the dangerous art of tightrope walking. Too bad she was such a pain on the ground.

"What's going on between you and Miranda?" Kristin whispered.

Prue wasn't sure if Kristin was asking as a journalist worried about antagonizing a subject or as a gossip wanting dirt.

"A simple misunderstanding," Prue said. She figured that was the safest answer. "What do you think is holding up Ivan's act?" she added, wanting to change the subject. Then it occurred to her—perhaps Miranda had detained Ivan.

Kristin shrugged. "I'll be sure to ask him." She gave Prue a sly glance. "Or maybe you can. You seem to have quite a rapport with the handsome Gypsy."

Now it was Prue who shrugged. She didn't want to encourage Kristin's speculation, or fuel Miranda's irritation. Miranda was throwing hostile glances in Prue's direction. Then her expression changed. Prue turned her head to see who Miranda was now gazing at so steadily.

Big surprise. Ivan hurried out of the dressing room area. He stalked straight to Miranda and they had a quick whispered conference. Judging from their body language, both were quite tense. Prue wondered what they were discussing. She hoped it wasn't her! She also hoped the tension wouldn't affect Ivan's performance. She knew that animals were very sensitive: they could pick up a person's anxieties. If the tigers, or bears, or lions sensed that Ivan was distracted, he could easily be put in danger.

"Ladies and gentlemen," boomed the ringmaster. "Now we present Ivan the Gypsy Violinist."

Ivan stepped away from Miranda and shut his eyes. He took a deep breath as the lighting changed. Then he placed the violin on his shoulder and lifted the bow. He held up his head and played the first, beautiful, plaintive note. He strode into the ring.

Prue moved into position. She kept her eyes focused intently on the violin. She didn't want Ivan's charisma to distract her from her goal. She had to take pictures of the back of that instrument. She raised the camera to her face. "Those symbols tell a story, Ivan," she murmured. "I need to know if that story is a tragedy."

CHAPTER
12

Prue knelt beside her equipment bag. She was fairly confident that she had gotten at least one clear shot of the symbols on the back of Ivan's violin. All around her there was bustling activity. The performance was over, but the ring was even more crowded as riggers and roustabouts and performers gathered up props and equipment. Children streamed down to ringside to talk to clowns, and staff members barked into walkie-talkies. It was some operation.

Ivan had vanished backstage the moment his act was over. So had Miranda. Ivan had told Prue that he always made sure his animals were comfortable and fed before coming back to clear out his dressing room area. Did Miranda help him with that task, or was tonight special? Something definitely was up with those two. Were they a couple fighting? Was Ivan actually Miranda's boyfriend and his flirting with Prue a serious no-no? Despite the gossip about Ivan, though, not a single circus performer accused him of being a womanizer or mentioned a relationship with Miranda. And some of them had been pretty forthcoming with romantic gossip about other performers! All they mentioned was bad luck. A few had described incidents, and some seemed downright hostile about Ivan's bad luck. If there was something between Miranda and Ivan that she was interfering with, Prue was pretty confident she would have heard something.

"I'm glad you're still here," a deep, accented voice said. Prue glanced up and gazed into Ivan's almond-shaped eyes. She felt herself go a little squooshy inside.

"The act was beautiful again," Prue complimented him. It was true. Whatever problem he and Miranda had been having before he entered the ring, Ivan was transformed the moment he began playing. So was the audience. Prue had felt the hush come over the crowd as Ivan's music soared and the wild beasts behaved like pussycats and teddy bears.

Ivan smiled shyly, his face crinkling into dimples. "I'm glad you think so. Listen, I wanted to ask you something."

Prue's heart thudded a little as she stood up. "Yes?"

"I was wondering if you would like to be my guest at a special performers' party. It is Kaboodle's birthday."

"I'd like that." Well, not the clown birthday party part, but Prue knew she would enjoy spending time with Ivan.

Ivan's smile broadened. "Wonderful. Why don't you meet me in front of my trailer around midnight."

"Isn't that kind of late?" Prue asked. She wondered what she would do with herself for the next few hours.

"I have something I must take care of first," Ivan explained. "And without me as your escort, the performers will never allow you to join the party. It's for insiders only."

Prue nodded. "I understand. Midnight it is."

"Prue," a stern voice called. Prue glanced over her shoulder. Piper, Phoebe, and Jenny stood nearby. Phoebe was the one who had spoken. Her arms were folded across her chest, and she was glaring at Ivan.

"In a minute," Prue called back.

"I'll leave you to your sisters," Ivan said. "Till midnight."

"Till midnight."

Ivan vanished into the backstage crowd.

"Did I hear right?" Kristin asked. "Did he just ask you to a party?"

"Yes." Prue snapped her case shut.

Kristin gave Prue a light punch on the shoulder. "You are so lucky! I am so jealous."

"It's just a party," Prue said. She wondered if Kristin had a crush on any of the performers. If she did, Prue figured it would have to be a clown.

"But it's on the inside," Kristin squealed. "That's so special—to have been invited to see how they really live. I wish I were going. Well, you'll just have to be my eyes and ears. Take notes, take pictures, if they let you!"

"I'll do my best," Prue promised, not very enthusiastically.

Kristin bounced off to talk to Mr. Amalfi the ring-master, and Prue went to face her sisters.

"So, ready to rock?" Piper asked.

"Well, actually, I'm going to hang around a bit longer."

"How much longer?" Phoebe asked. "And why?"

"Ivan asked me to a party. I told him I'd go." Prue didn't meet her sisters' eyes. She knew they would go ballistic.

"You can't!" Jenny exclaimed. "Olga said Ivan brings trouble to those who care about him."

Now, here's a tricky situation, Prue mused. Can I tell Jenny not to believe such nonsense when I'm a witch myself?

She tried to laugh it off. "I can take care of myself," she promised Jenny.

"Can you?" Piper asked. "You are kind of smitten and that can cloud your judgment."

"I don't get what you see in him," Phoebe declared. "Okay, he has a good act, but other than that, I don't see any redeeming qualities whatsoever."

"I—I can't explain it," Prue said truthfully. There was something different about Ivan.

"I can. I think I've figured out what's—" Phoebe glared at Piper, who gripped her arm. "What?"

"I don't think we should go into this now. Here."

Phoebe glanced at Jenny, who luckily was watching Mitzi trying to round up her performing poodles. "Okay," she said quietly. "But you be careful. And Piper and I will be doing some serious research into all this."

"I need to get Jenny home, it's way past her bed-time," Piper said. "You be careful."

"I promise." Prue watched her sisters leave with Jenny. She had about an hour or so to kill before meeting Ivan. She figured the best thing she could do was stay out of the way. She picked up her bag and carefully threaded through the crew and the equipment surrounding her.

She made her way over to the seats and plopped into the second row. Crews were sweeping the ring and setting up the tent for the next day's performance.

A few seats away a man with a clipboard sat scribbling notes and talking into his headset. "We need more blue gels, the two on the left are fried. Also, that cue during the contortionist bit is a little early. And the band needs to pay closer attention to Miranda. Her performance deserves their one hundred percent support. The flute should be following her arm movements."

Prue was impressed that even though the show was up and running, notes were taken every night to make sure the high level of quality was maintained.

"What happened with the clowns? Who was late? Well, find out," the man said sternly.

So it was a mistake, Prue noted. Once again, she was struck by the professionalism of the clowns—despite their being clowns. Not a single audience member had been aware that anything was wrong. Although different, the act had been as entertaining as it had been the night before.

A startling odor made Prue's nose wrinkle. Sweat, cigarettes, and something unidentifiable wafted her way.

"What am I doing wrong?" Raphael the Tattooed

Snake Charmer leaned onto the back of the seat beside Prue. He was sitting in the row behind her. The unidentifiable odor must be eau de snake, Prue realized.

"I am sorely in need of advice," Raphael continued. "I've used all of my sure-fire lady-killers to get your sister Phoebe's attention. Nothing seems to have worked."

Prue bit her lip to keep from laughing. She'd seen Raphael in action and wouldn't have imagined any of his attempts to court Phoebe as "lady-killers." Chasing a girl around with a large boa constrictor didn't strike Prue as the way to anyone's heart. Though, she admitted, if it would work on any of the Halliwells, Phoebe would be the one.

"I've never seen such a sweet, pretty thing as that there Phoebe. And Isabella, my snake, seems to agree. She let Phoebe pet her without any fuss at all. Am I losing my touch? Am I no longer the good-looker?"

Prue studied Raphael's crooked face, complete with missing teeth and neck tattoos. The man seemed so genuinely perplexed that Prue decided to let him down easy.

"I'm sure it isn't you," Prue told him. "Phoebe isn't really in the market for a boyfriend. Particularly one who will be leaving town soon."

Raphael stroked his stubbly chin. "You know, you may have something there. The circus life isn't for every woman. What if she fell hard? This is just the start of the tour. I'll be on the road for the next six months."

"Exactly. She's just protecting herself from a broken heart."

Raphael nodded slowly. "I wouldn't want to do anything to hurt that young lady," he said. "I'd better turn off the charm."

If you could get past his tough-guy looks and his rather overpowering smell, Raphael really was kind of sweet.

"Is there a reason you're still here, miss?" Raphael gave her a sidelong glance. "As if I didn't already know. These old peepers see plenty."

"I-I've been invited to Kaboodle's birthday party," Prue explained.

"That's quite an invite. Someone must really like you."

Prue felt herself flush. Was there a lot of gossiping going on about her and Ivan? That couldn't make Miranda happy.

"And where is our handsome Gypsy?" Raphael continued. "Or is his bad luck keeping him from making his appointment on time?"

Another reference to Ivan's bad luck. "No, he told me he had something to take care of first. Maybe with the animals?"

Raphael shrugged. "I'm going to head over to Clown Alley. I don't want all the cake to be gone. The party must have already started."

Prue checked her watch. It was nearly midnight. "It's time for me to meet Ivan. I'll go with you."

They strolled out of the tent. Once they were in the fresh night air, Raphael's rather significant personal perfume faded to a more bearable level. He flicked on a flashlight.

In the weak beam, shadows danced all around. The famous tall trees of Golden Gate Park blocked any illumination that might have come from the stars or the moon. The street lamps were placed very far apart, since usually there weren't nighttime events in the park. Prue shivered.

"Why don't I walk with you," Raphael offered. "I don't like the idea of you strolling around here without a flashlight."

"Thanks." Prue was grateful. She spotted Ivan's trailer up ahead. A light was on inside.

"Oh, good," Prue said. "He must be here already."

"I'll just wait to be sure, missy," Raphael said.

They approached Ivan's trailer. A sudden loud bang made Prue jump. An explosion!

Ivan's trailer burst into flames!

CHAPTER
13

"Oh, my god," Prue gasped. She stood frozen, staring at the orange-and-blue flames leaping into the air.

Raphael let out a cry, bellowing "Fire!" He charged forward, without any thought to his own safety. "I'll find the gas lines!"

Within moments, it seemed, the area was crawling with circus people. Even though Clown Alley was on the other side of the tent, Prue was amazed to see how quickly everyone got there. Several people showed up with fire extinguishers.

"Soak the trees!" someone shouted.

Prue looked up. The flames were leaping so high the overhanging trees were in danger of catching fire. If that happened, the whole park could go up. The weather had been particularly dry, and the trees' branches were close together.

Flames licked higher and higher, rising ever closer to the bottommost branches. Prue studied the huge tree shading Ivan's trailer. The next highest branch was quite far up. Prue focused her energy. She concentrated on the branch and with a quick and subtle flick of her hand, cracked off the branch and tossed it far from the fire.

Chaos reigned all around her. People were shouting encouragement, screaming in fear, calling out orders. Everywhere Prue turned she saw an opportunity to use her telekinesis to help. Things were so crazy she had no worry that anyone would notice or connect her hand waves to any of the actions around her. She helped hoist a heavy hose into position atop several performers' shoulders. She moved a small child out of harm's way. She whirled around just in time to alter the course of shards of glass as a window shattered from the heat.

Smoke poured out of the broken trailer windows. Prue diverted its direction, trying desperately to peer through the smoke. The terrifying question kept pounding in her heart: Is Ivan still inside?

Then her body flooded with relief. She spotted Ivan stomping out flames by the trailer door.

With the fire beginning to subside, and knowing that Ivan was safe, Prue began to tune into her surroundings. At some point, firefighters had arrived on the scene. She had never even noticed. They pushed all the circus folk away, to the sidelines, to allow them to do their job.

The firefighters streamed in and out of the terribly damaged trailer. Suddenly EMS workers swarmed toward the trailer with a stretcher.

Someone was inside, Prue realized with horror. Could the person possibly have survived the blaze?

A cry went up, along with murmurs and gasps. "Miranda."

Miranda had been in Ivan's trailer. Yet Ivan had been outside, alive. What did this mean? Prue wondered.

All around her, gossip flew. "Poor Miranda," a large woman said. "She always refused to see that Ivan simply didn't feel about her the way she felt about him."

"I heard he asked her to meet him here, to put an end to her nonsense once and for all," a gruff voice added. "She'd become a nuisance."

"This is more of Ivan's bad luck," the clown Prue remembered from the first day—Sacha—said. He was standing with Olga. "Just coming into contact with him brings trouble."

"That's ridiculous," Kaboodle protested. "There must have been a problem with the gas line."

"There's nothing supernatural going on here," Masha agreed.

"Foolish," Olga muttered. "Foolish and blind. All of you. Him, too. He refused my help. You should insist he take my offer."

"I think Ivan should just leave," another person said. "We're all in danger with him around."

"We'd all be out of jobs then," Kaboodle countered. "He's the biggest draw, and we're not doing that well as it is."

Prue's head swam. She didn't know what to make of all of these comments. If Phoebe's vision was right, and Ivan really was capable of trying to strangle Piper, could he also have deliberately trapped Miranda in that fire? Could that be what he needed to take care of before meeting me?

Prue shook her head. The thought was too awful.

She peered toward the trailer. The EMS workers had taken off in the ambulance, and the firefighters were now allowing Ivan to enter the trailer. The fire must have been completely out. Prue moved closer. Could anything be salvaged from that inferno? She'd never seen anything like it. The fire happened so fast. Was it the work of a demon? And was Ivan that demon? She hadn't been able to see him close up enough to check out his reaction to the news of Miranda's death.

Ivan came back out of the trailer, a stunned expression on his sooty face. He stood clutching his violin. Astonishingly, it had survived the fire. In fact, from where Prue stood, it looked as if the violin wasn't even singed.

Did Ivan magically protect his precious instrument and not a human life? Or did the violin protect itself?

Prue's stomach was tied in knots. The fire, the questions, Ivan's guilt or innocence, Miranda's death—it was suddenly all too much. Without even a glance back at the handsome Gypsy, Prue hurried away from the disturbing scene.

"My eyes are seeing double," Phoebe complained. "Double basses. Triple clefs, and far too many quarter notes."

"And you claimed you weren't musical," Piper quipped. She shut her eyes and rubbed them. She let out a yawn. "Let's take a break."

Ever since they'd come home from the circus, Piper and Phoebe had been up in the attic going through *The Book of Shadows*. They had found a lot of information about magic and music. Music used in spells and also magical instruments. Pages and pages of magical instruments.

Phoebe kept trying to keep herself from thinking about Prue being alone with Ivan this late and on his turf.

Piper continued poring over the pages of *The Book of Shadows*. "Look at all these powers," she said. "There are instruments to make people fall in or out of love. To control the weather. To ward off psychic attacks." She sighed. "But without knowing all the symbols, we can't interpret the kind of power Ivan's violin might have."

Phoebe drummed a rhythm with her fingertips on the table. "I know that violin is being used for something," Phoebe said. "I just hope it isn't to cast a spell over Prue."

Phoebe told Piper her theory that the reason Prue was uncharacteristically gaga over the Gypsy was because said Gypsy had cast a spell on her. Maybe with the violin.

"Could be," Piper mused. "Here's the good news, though," she added with excitement.

"There's good news? Finally." Phoebe slid beside Piper. "Where? Show me good news."

Piper pointed to a passage in *The Book of Shadows*. " 'Many of the spells of these instruments may be neutralized by the Power of Three,' " she read. "At least we have a chance."

"Mmm." Phoebe thought a moment. "Does Ivan know there are three of us?"

"I can't remember," Piper admitted. "But given

how chummy he and Prue are I'd guess that the
answer is yes. Olga seemed awfully interested in us,
so the number three must be important in Gypsy
magic, too."

Phoebe nodded. She absently flipped through the
pages of *The Book of Shadows*. She was so tired, but
she didn't want to go to bed without finding some
answers first. Sometimes, if she let go just enough,
the book itself would lead them to just what they
needed to know. Sometimes Phoebe had the feeling
that the book was teaching them about their powers.
She also felt as if their mother was somehow watching over them through the book. Phoebe had been so
young when her mother had died that she barely
remembered her. But it was her mother who had
written many of the spells in the book. And it was
through her mother, and her mother's mother, and
all those mother's mothers before them that Phoebe
and her sister got their powers. So when a page
would flutter, or the book would fall naturally to a
particular spell, Phoebe felt as if it was guided by her
mother's watchful hand.

She felt that way now. Her fingers stopped at a
specific page, smoothing it out without even thinking. She looked down.

A ghoulish figure gazed up at her from the book.

"Ick," she commented. "Who is this dude?"

Piper leaned in to stare at the picture. "Hey," she
said. "Doesn't he look as if he's wearing a Gypsy outfit?"

"Yeah, only it really needs to swing by the laun-
dromat." There was no text on the page, just the picture. Phoebe studied it carefully. The figure wore the

full pants and colorful vest and scarves of a traditional Gypsy outfit. But this Gypsy's face was decaying, as if it had been long dead. Tattered strips of fabric hung from the figure's outstretched arms. Its fingers were skeletal, and its eyes were hollow sockets.

"Didn't Prue say she saw someone looking like this sneaking around the circus?" Phoebe said.

Piper's eyes widened. "She did! Does the book explain what this thing is?"

Phoebe flipped the page. Sure enough, there was the text to accompany the picture. " 'Gypsy Zombie,' " Phoebe read. "Wow. It says here that a powerful Gypsy magician can call up a zombie to do his or her dirty work! That way the Gypsy can remain above reproach and still get what he or she wants."

"Does it say what kinds of things a Gypsy might ask the zombie to do?" Piper asked.

"You mean a zombie job description? Let me see. Yeah, it's quite a list. All the biggies: Kidnapping, murder, burglary. Hey—wait. Some are pretty intense—and weird."

"Being murdered by a zombie isn't weird enough?" Piper asked.

"For a truly skilled magician, the zombie can be used to do your bidding on the astral plane. This is important if you need to battle psychic attacks. It is also useful in searching for additional powerful talismans, such as the Romany ruby and other charged objects."

"Romany ruby?" Piper interrupted. "That was the gem that gave Gypsies threefold power. Ivan told

Phoebe about it, but he claimed he didn't believe in it."

"Sure. And he claims he's Mr. Nice Guy, too, only I know different," Phoebe said. She still couldn't figure out what Prue saw in the guy.

"Olga sure seemed to believe in it," Piper remembered. "Jenny mentioned the ruby, and Olga just about freaked that Gypsy secrets were being spread to us non-Gypsies."

"Uh-oh," Phoebe said, reading further. "I think I just figured out why there's Gypsy magic in our *Book of Shadows*. The zombie may also be of use in fighting the neutralizing powers of the Charmed Ones."

"Oh, goodie. Why is there always a catch?" Piper said. She rubbed her face.

"I guess the question is, what is Ivan using the zombie to do?" Phoebe said.

"Are we absolutely sure it's Ivan who has conjured the zombie?" Piper asked. "We really have to keep an open mind."

"Why? An open mind just might get Prue—or you—killed!" Phoebe knew on some level that Piper was right—that she might be jumping to conclusions. Still, Ivan hadn't won her over into his fan club. Someone had to keep some perspective around that guy.

"All I'm saying is, maybe someone has conjured up the zombie to harm Ivan," Piper replied. "We still haven't ruled out the idea that he's cursed."

Phoebe let out a huge yawn. "Sorry," she said sheepishly. "I think I'd better hit the sack. I'm too tired to put any pieces together at all anymore."

"Thank goodness," Piper said. "I was hoping

you'd say that. I didn't want to seem like a wimp and poop out first."

Phoebe placed the book back on its stand. Thanks, Mom, she thought, holding her hand on the book's cover for a long moment. Then she slung her arm over Piper's shoulders. "Come along, fellow party-pooper. Let's get some shut-eye."

They headed back downstairs. "No use waiting up for Prue if that party doesn't even start until midnight," Piper said. "There's no telling when she'll get home."

"If she'll get home," Phoebe grumbled. She so did not trust Ivan.

Piper stopped in her tracks. "Why did you have to say that?" she demanded. "Now I'll never get to sleep."

"Sorry, sorry." Phoebe pushed Piper along the hallway to their rooms. She stopped at her door. "Let's just hope it's Ivan's charm and not his evil plans that will keep Prue out all night."

"I'm with you on that," Piper said with a deep sigh.

CHAPTER
14

Piper sat up in bed with a start. Had she been dreaming? Something about Prue . . . Then she remembered. She never heard Prue come home last night.

Piper leaped out of bed and scurried to Prue's room. She didn't even bother to knock, she just flung open the door. Yes! Prue's bed was definitely slept in.

Wait a sec. Did Prue ever make her bed yesterday? They had left the house in such a hurry. It was possible those rumpled sheets were from the night before.

Piper dashed downstairs. Phoebe was sitting at the table, eating cereal. "Did she come home?" Piper demanded.

"Note," Phoebe said, her mouth full. "Counter."

"Not had your full quota of coffee yet?" Piper asked. Phoebe grunted a reply and reached for her coffee cup.

Piper found the note. "Oh, my goodness!" Piper exclaimed. "A fire?"

Phoebe nodded grimly. "Just like in my vision."

Piper scanned the note quickly. Prue explained that Kristin had scheduled an early meeting. Because of the fire, the carnival would be crawling with reporters, so she wanted to be there first thing. Prue also asked Piper and Phoebe to please stay home and said that she'd try to be back early to fill them in on everything.

" 'Please don't worry,' " Piper read from the note. She shook the paper at Phoebe. "As if."

Phoebe took another swig of coffee. "There's no way that we're staying here. I'm convinced our big sister is in danger."

Panic crossed Piper's face. "She did come home, didn't she?" Piper asked. "This isn't some kind of magical bogus note?"

"Don't think so. There was a coffee cup in the sink when I got up, and Prue's hair conditioner was sitting on the edge of the shower. She was here." Phoebe gave a sharp, decisive nod. "And now we're going there."

"Spoken like a fully caffeinated witch." Piper grabbed some OJ from the fridge. She knocked back a swig.

"From the carton?" Phoebe asked, incredulous. "You must be worried."

Piper replaced the carton and shut the fridge. "We need to know what she knows, and she needs to know what we know. You know?"

"I know. I mean, I think I know." Phoebe's brow furrowed. "What did you say?"

Piper shook her head. "Never mind. Let's just go."

The girls dressed in a hurry. Piper grabbed her coat from the hook in the front hall. "Phoebe?" Piper called. "You ready?"

"In a minute!" Phoebe's voice came from somewhere upstairs. In a few minutes, she bounded down the stairs, tucking a piece of paper into the pocket of her pants.

"What's that?" Piper asked.

"A little protection." She patted her pocket. "I copied down the spell for fighting off that zombie. We may run into him."

"Good thinking."

The doorbell rang. "Are we expecting anyone?" Piper whispered.

"I don't think Gypsy zombies ring doorbells," Phoebe said.

Piper peered through the lace curtains hanging beside the front door. "Jenny," she said. She swung open the door and gazed at the girl's eager expression.

"Are we going back to the carnival?" Jenny asked.

Piper sighed. "Well, *we* are," she told Jenny. "But we just can't bring you with us."

Jenny's face fell. "You—you don't want me tagging along anymore, is that it?"

"No, of course not, sweetie," Piper assured the girl. "There was a terrible accident there last night. It's not safe."

"Oh." Jenny looked disappointed but a lot less hurt. That's a relief, Piper thought. One less thing to feel guilty about.

Phoebe and Piper drove to the park. By now the

security guard at the back entrance recognized them and waved them right through. They had formulated something resembling a plan on the drive over. Phoebe would try to find Prue while Piper conferred with Olga. The fortune-teller might be of use. She could shed some light on the zombie, Ivan, everything.

Piper and Phoebe arrived at the grove where Olga stationed her vardo. "I'll bring Prue back here," Phoebe promised.

"Assuming you find her and she agrees to come with you," Piper pointed out. "We have no idea what's really going on with Ivan."

"You're right," Phoebe agreed. "We may need to cast a reversal spell if Ivan is using some kind of charm on her."

Phoebe gave Piper's hand a quick squeeze, then headed in the direction of the tent. Piper turned to face Olga's colorful wagon. Olga had been pretty vocal about the curse on Ivan. Piper hoped the woman's concerns would make her willing to talk about what she believed about Ivan. If she could, Piper intended to avoid revealing that she was a witch, though she suspected Olga had already sensed that about her.

"Olga?" Piper called.

Olga popped her head out through the curtain hanging across the front door of the wagon. "Ah, the young lady with the two sisters."

"Hello," Piper said. "Actually, it's because of one of those sisters that I wanted to see you," Piper said.

Olga's eyes narrowed and she nodded slowly. "Come in," she said.

Piper followed Olga into the dark wagon. Piper's nose crinkled a little. An acrid, smoky odor hung heavily in the air. Olga must have been making potions or charms, Piper thought. Jars sat open on the shelves, and herbs crunched under Piper's feet as she crossed to the table. Olga isn't the tidiest practitioner, she observed.

Olga gestured for Piper to sit at the table. "It has been a terrible day," she said, sinking into the chair opposite Piper. "Have you heard about Miranda? Oh, so sad. Such a shame. It is all that Ivan's fault."

That caught Piper's attention. Olga certainly opened the door for questions about Ivan. Piper cleared her throat, finding it hard to breathe freely in the close atmosphere. Something smelled like it had been dead for a few days. Piper wondered how frequently Olga took out the garbage. "How is it Ivan's fault?" she choked out.

Olga slapped the table. "Why, the evil that is upon him, of course!" she exclaimed.

"That's what I wanted to talk to you about," Piper said. "My sister Prue seems very, well, attached to Ivan."

Olga threw her thick arms into the air. "Then her very soul is at stake. He shall destroy her as he destroyed Miranda."

Could Ivan have been responsible for Miranda's death? Piper wondered. So far, Olga hadn't been very forthcoming with exactly how Ivan accomplished his evil deeds. Piper opened her mouth to ask Olga for some specifics when the fortune-teller clutched Piper's arm.

"I am so relieved that you have come to see me," Olga said.

Piper tried not to flinch in Olga's powerful grip. "Why?"

"I saw Ivan luring your sister into a secluded area, behind the carnival." She released Piper's arm and made a sign against the evil eye. "Who knows what he plans for her?"

"Oh, no!" Piper gasped.

"I would have tried to stop him," Olga said, wringing her hands. "But I am old and weak. No match for his evil. But you—you are young and strong." She leaned across the table toward Piper. "You have power!"

Piper was startled both by Olga's choice of the word "power" and by the woman's intensity. Although Olga didn't seem at all frail, Piper figured she was so afraid of Ivan's magic that she didn't see herself as a match for him.

"Which way did they go?" Piper asked. Olga gave Piper directions to the path where she had last seen Ivan and Prue and where she thought he might be taking her.

"Thank you," Piper said, rising from her seat.

"I only hope you are not too late," Olga moaned.

Piper hoped so, too. She dashed out of the vardo, blinking in the bright sunlight. Her head whipped around, searching out Phoebe.

There she was—running straight toward her! The sisters charged at each other.

"I couldn't find Prue anywhere," Phoebe blurted. She bent forward and placed her hands on her knees, catching her breath.

"That's because Ivan has her!" Piper exclaimed. "Olga told me where he took her."

Phoebe straightened up. "Let's book."

Piper led Phoebe along a rutted path, leading into the wooded area of the park. The foliage was so thick that the trees and bushes blocked out some of the sounds from the carnival.

Piper shuddered. Today the park seemed dark and sinister. The first day of the carnival had seemed so bright and cheerful. She remembered how carefree she had felt just a few days ago. Sort of the way she had felt before coming into her power as a witch, she realized. Being a witch was such a responsibility and had brought so much darkness into her life.

It had brought great joy, too, Piper reminded herself. Rescuing an innocent, setting things right, bonding with her sisters—these were all the good side of being a witch. But times like these—being put into danger, not knowing if this would be the day the magic failed, or if they would finally be confronted by a more powerful demon, a trickier warlock—these were the times when Piper wished she and her sisters had never found *The Book of Shadows.*

She glanced at Phoebe jogging beside her. Phoebe had taken most easily to the knowledge. She was growing in her spell casting and developing her ability to have visions. Prue, too, had been expanding her skills. In addition to telekinesis, Prue had discovered her ability to astral project. Well, if anyone could find a way to be in two places at once, Piper thought, it would be her big sister, Prue.

"Shouldn't we have found them by now?" Phoebe asked.

"Should be soon," Piper promised. "Olga was sure Ivan was taking Prue to a clearing just around that bend up ahead."

"Do you smell something weird?" Phoebe asked. "Like dead fish?"

Piper nodded. "I was trying not to notice."

A figure in the bushes caught Piper's eye. She grabbed Phoebe's arm and pulled her to a stop. "Is that Ivan?" she whispered.

"I don't know," Phoebe replied.

Before they could discern the figure's identity, it crashed out of the bushes, trailing branches and leaves. It reached out its long bony fingers as it stalked toward the sisters.

"The zombie," Piper murmured.

"I think we've discovered the source of that funky stink," Phoebe commented. "That guy's been dead for a while."

Piper stared at the zombie as it moved toward them. Her stomach clenched as her eyes traveled up its tattered clothing to its horrifying skull-like face. Her insides twisted even more as she gazed at the figure's hollow eye sockets and its peeling skin.

"What are you waiting for?" Phoebe squeezed Piper's elbow. "Time freeze him."

"Right!" Piper snapped out of it. She flicked her fingers at the zombie, sending the freezing energy out of her hands.

He took another lurching step toward them.

"It didn't work!" Piper gasped. She turned frightened eyes to Phoebe. She saw her terror mirrored in her sister's expression. "You just can't predict dead guys," Phoebe quipped.

Piper knew Phoebe's feeble joke was an attempt to mask her fear. "Now what?"

"Three . . ." the zombie rasped. Its hollow, rumbling voice sounded to Piper as if it came from some other world. The zombie took another step.

"Spell!" Piper exclaimed. "You have a spell!"

"Right!" Phoebe cried. She rummaged through her pockets. "Where did I put it?"

Piper searched Phoebe's many jacket pockets. "Why are multiple pockets in this season?" she muttered. Phoebe twisted and turned, checking each of her shirt and pants pockets.

"Hurry," Piper urged. "If he gets any closer I'm going to pass out from the stench before he has a chance to kill us."

Phoebe held up a tiny slip of paper. "Got it!" she cheered.

The zombie was now close enough for Piper to see the insects crawling all over it—in its ears, its mouth, its eye sockets. Oh, man, Piper thought. We need to do this spell quick, before I hurl.

"Three," the zombie intoned again, only this time Piper thought it sounded more like a question.

"Shut up," Phoebe snapped at the zombie. She and Piper huddled close so they could both read the spell. "Go," she ordered Piper. Piper nodded. Together they chanted:

"Minion of darkness, ancient Gypsy tool
   Sent for destruction, mindless yet cruel,
   We break your commands,
   We shatter your rules."

Piper glanced at Phoebe. "That's kind of mean, isn't it? The mindless bit?"

"Again!" Phoebe ordered. "Put everything into it. It might work only with the Power of Three."

They repeated the chant over and over, their voices rising, their pace quickening. Each time they said the spell, Piper could feel it grow in power.

The zombie swayed, its hollow eye sockets locked on their faces as if it could see out of those empty holes. As their voices got louder, stronger, more urgent, the zombie began to break apart. Its body collapsed in on itself, as if it were hollow inside. The shell of the zombie caved in, until all that was left was a pile of foul-smelling dust.

Piper and Phoebe stood holding hands, breathing hard, staring at the spot where only moments ago the zombie had stood, bearing down on them. Phoebe slipped the spell back into her pants pocket. "This time I'll remember where I put it," she promised.

Something puzzled Piper. "The zombie seemed confused that there weren't three of us," she said, nodding slowly. "It was sent to destroy us so that the Power of Three would be neutralized."

"We lucked out because we didn't match its programming," Phoebe realized. "So the spell worked even without Prue."

Phoebe and Piper gaped at each other. "Prue!" they cried in unison.

"We have to get going!" Piper declared. "The zombie may have been sent to delay us from saving Prue from Ivan."

The two girls raced toward the bend in the road. Piper was certain that was where they'd find Prue.

If they weren't too late.

"Almost there," Piper panted.

They careened around a large oak tree, its broad spreading limbs seeming to reach out at them. They skidded to a stop on the dirt path.

"Uh, Piper?" Phoebe said quietly.

"Yes, I see," Piper replied.

No Ivan. No Prue.

Just a great big tiger!

CHAPTER
15

Purely on instinct Piper threw up her hands and willed the tiger to stop.

The powerful creature froze midleap. Piper gave a quick thanks that her power had worked on the animal. After the run-in with the zombie she wasn't sure it would.

She stared at the tiger. Its massive front paws reached out, claws extended. Its mouth was stretched back in a hideous grimace, its sharp teeth looking deadly and huge. Piper knew that if she hadn't frozen the creature in time, she and Phoebe would be tiger treats right now.

They might still wind up snack food! Piper's heart thudded as she saw another tiger creeping forward. Its belly was low to the ground as it approached stealthily. Any moment now the creature would pounce. Piper channeled her energy and sent the freeze out of her fingers toward the tiger. It froze, crouched low.

"Piper! Over there!" Phoebe grabbed Piper's arm and pointed toward another pathway. One of Ivan's bears was lumbering toward them. It threw back its head and let out an angry roaring growl. Piper froze it.

The air in front of her wavered. The first tiger was unfreezing. She zapped it again, then whirled to freeze the second tiger. Just in time she noticed a movement behind her. Without even looking to see the attacker, she sent a freeze over her shoulder.

Phoebe glanced back. "A lion," she gasped. "These are all of Ivan's animals! They've been set loose!"

"And they don't stay frozen!" Piper wailed. She refroze the bear. "They must have some kind of protective charm on them. Keep your eyes out for any more," she ordered Phoebe. "I can't remember how many animals Ivan has!"

Phoebe stood with her back to Piper. "I've got this direction covered."

Another bear crashed through the bushes, and Piper froze it. She could tell her power was weakening. She was getting exhausted. She had never had to freeze so many creatures at once, over and over. How much longer could she keep going?

"Where's Prue?" Phoebe asked. "Are we too late? Did Ivan feed her to the animals?"

"I don't know," Piper replied. "I can't think about it. I need to concentrate. *You* think about how we're going to get out of here in one piece." She refroze the tigers again, then turned and caught the lion.

Voices! Piper heard two familiar voices back in the

woods. Prue and Ivan. Her heart started pounding again. Is this where Phoebe's vision comes true? Is Ivan going to strangle me?

Ivan and Prue were coming toward the clearing from a path off the side, away from the ones the animals were using. Ivan was luring Prue here to have the animals maul her, Piper realized. We weren't too late—we were too early! He must have taken her the long way around. Probably pretending this was some nice romantic stroll. Ha!

Prue and Ivan sauntered out from among the trees.

"Prue, run!" Piper shrieked.

A look of shock crossed Ivan's face. Piper wasted no time. She froze him.

"Prue, go!" Phoebe yelled. "It's feeding time at the zoo!"

"What—" Prue's eyes flicked from frozen animal to frozen animal.

"I can't keep them frozen," Piper shouted. "Get out of here."

"Not a chance," Prue declared.

The air around Ivan wavered. Piper knew her depleted energy must be affecting her freezing power. "Keep an eye on Ivan," Piper told Phoebe. "You may have to take him out the old-fashioned way. I have to keep dealing with the animals."

Phoebe assumed a karate stance as Ivan unfroze. He stared at the animals posed all around them. The lion began to shudder, and Piper instantly froze it again.

"What have you done?" Ivan cried. "What are you doing?" He hurled himself toward Piper.

"Back off!" Prue pointed her finger at him and sent him flying into the bushes. She turned back to her sisters. "Now!" she shouted.

The three Halliwells grabbed hands and raced away from the clearing.

Please don't follow us, Piper prayed silently. She didn't think she had any energy left in her to contend with those beasts.

The sisters didn't slow their pace or dare to look back. Prue led Piper and Phoebe through the least populated areas of the carnival. People, booths, scenery all flew by Piper in a blur.

No one spoke a word until they were in Prue's car. The moment they were buckled up, Prue peeled out of the lot and headed for home.

"Now do you believe me?" Phoebe demanded. "Ivan is bad news."

"It sure looks that way," Prue admitted.

Piper could hear the disappointment in her sister's voice. She knew how hard it was to hear that someone you trusted wasn't who you thought he was. Not only did it hurt, it made you doubt your own judgment, and that never felt good.

"I think there was some kind of antiwitch charm on those animals," Piper added. "It may have been very general, so it didn't block me completely, but it definitely cramped my style."

"Ivan didn't know exactly what sort of power to protect against," Phoebe suggested. "One size doesn't fit all in magic spells."

"But what is he after?" Prue said. She banged the steering wheel, then turned into their driveway. "What could he possibly want?"

Phoebe shrugged. "What does any demon or war-lock want? Us dead."

Piper shot Phoebe a warning glance and tipped her head toward Prue. Sometimes Phoebe could be a little insensitive.

"What?" Phoebe demanded. "I know that sounded harsh, but it's the truth."

Prue sighed as she parked. "Sorry, guys. I put us all in danger. He just seems so . . . so not warlock."

"I know, sweetie," Piper said sympathetically. "And we actually don't really know what's going on. It is still possible that Ivan himself is under some kind of curse."

"I'm just really glad that my vision still hasn't come true." Phoebe climbed out of the car. Piper and Prue followed her up the walk.

"Only one of the visions has," Prue reminded her. "The fire."

"That hairbrush must have belonged to Miranda," Phoebe realized. "Instead of seeing her, it was as if I became her." She shuddered. "How horrible for the poor girl."

Piper wondered if Ivan was responsible for the tragic death. From the look on Prue's face, she knew her sister was wondering the same thing.

"Well, these photos should clear up some of our questions," Prue said. "At least about the magic of the violin."

Prue's tone told Piper she was trying very hard to mask her hurt and concern. She was working dou-ble-time at being the strong, efficient Prue.

"So let's get to it," Piper said. She knew Prue would feel better if she was doing something, taking action.

They went down to the darkroom. While they waited for the enlargements to develop, Phoebe and Piper filled Prue in on what they had discovered in *The Book of Shadows* the previous day.

"So it could be that Ivan channels his power through the violin?" Prue asked.

"Or the violin may have its own power and is using it to channel Ivan," Piper suggested. She almost wished she hadn't said that. The flicker of hope that appeared in Prue's eyes at the thought that perhaps Ivan wasn't evil made it clear how much this situation was costing her.

"What we need to figure out is what the symbols mean," Piper said. "How they work together to create the specific magic of this violin. That's the only way we'll know how to stop him."

Prue paced the room as they waited for the pictures to develop. She kept checking the trays, the timer, then the trays again.

"Can't you hurry the process up, somehow?" Phoebe asked. "They don't need to be perfect. It's not like they're going to press or anything."

"Actually, they do need to be perfect," Prue countered. "We can't risk misinterpreting any of the symbols with blurry images."

"You're right," Phoebe said with a sigh. "Too bad I don't know any hurry-up-already spells."

"Not much longer," Prue promised. She moved photos from the developing solution into the washing trays.

Piper thought back to what they had learned about Gypsy magic. There had been a Gypsy zombie lurking around. A violin that appeared and disappeared. A whole system of love spells. A legend about a magic gem that granted power. A fortune-teller who was afraid of Ivan.

Maybe Ivan is trying to steal Olga's powers, Piper reasoned, the way warlocks try to steal power from us. That would give her cause for fear. There was definitely some kind of connection between those two, but Piper wasn't sure what.

"They're ready," Prue announced. Piper and Phoebe crowded around the trays as Prue lifted the first picture out of the solution with a pair of tongs.

"Good clear shot," Piper commented. "We should be able to match these images up pretty easily with the examples in *The Book of Shadows*."

Phoebe glanced into the tray. "What are the other photos of?" she asked.

"I was able to get pictures in Ivan's dressing room of the carvings in the bow," Prue said. "I blew them up, too, to make them easier to read."

One by one, Prue pulled the enlargements from the development solution and clipped them up to dry. Piper and Phoebe studied them carefully.

"Hey, wait a sec," Phoebe muttered.

"What?" Piper asked.

Phoebe held a photograph delicately between her fingers, being careful not to smudge the still-drying picture. "These were shot in Ivan's dressing room?" Phoebe asked.

"Yes, he was getting ready for the performance," Prue said.

"Is that clock right?" Phoebe asked.

"I suppose so. I didn't check it or anything," Prue answered. "Why?"

"There are shots of his watch in these performance pictures," Piper said. "Do you want to check the time in these?"

"Yes." Phoebe joined Piper and peered at the photograph.

"Okay, so it says eight o'clock on the clock in the dressing room," Phoebe said. "Let's assume it's close to being accurate. It says eight-ten on Ivan's watch when he's in the ring. Again, for argument's sake let's assume that's also basically right."

"It should be—there's a time stamp on the film for that roll," Prue said. "It's for taking action shots."

"Well, something is very weird here," Phoebe said. "Because I know for a fact that at eight-ten Ivan was screaming in my face."

There was a moment of silence as Piper glanced back and forth between her sisters. They all gaped at each other, wondering what this new bit of information meant.

"I—I never left his side," Prue declared.

"Even if you weren't around to verify his alibi," Phoebe said, "he never would have had the time to read me the riot act and still be onstage at eight-ten unless Piper and I both had set our watches wrong."

"Let me think . . ." Prue's eyes narrowed. Piper could tell her sister was flipping through her mental hard drive. "I set my watch by Ivan's dressing-room clock earlier in the afternoon."

"And I asked you the time before we split up!" Piper exclaimed. "Then gave you the time!" she added to Phoebe.

"We were all in sync with Ivan," Phoebe finished. "These times are accurate, all right."

"So, somehow, Ivan was in the ring performing and in his trailer yelling at Phoebe at the same time," Piper said. She turned to Prue. "Do you think he can astral project like you?"

"I don't think so, but I don't really know." Prue shrugged. "This whole time I haven't spotted any supernatural qualities in him. Only in the violin."

Phoebe paced the tiny space. "Could he have a twin?"

"How would we not notice a guy who looks exactly like him running around? And he would have mentioned it," Prue said. "He's told me a good deal about his family."

"And someone at the circus would have said something," Phoebe added. "Gossip flies around that place."

"Maybe no one knows," Piper suggested. "Including Ivan."

"You mean there's a second, secret Ivan?" Phoebe raised a skeptical eyebrow. "Do you think that's who's causing all of Ivan's bad luck? And the twin is the person I saw strangle you in my vision? Kind of dubious."

"I think it sounds more like Jekyll and Hyde," Prue commented. "As much as I hate to say it, are we sure we're talking about two different men?"

"You have the evidence right in your hands," Piper said. "Unless he can astral project, there seems to be two of them: a good Ivan and a bad Ivan."

"Well, we aren't going to solve this standing here. Time to do some more research," Phoebe said.

"Maybe the violin can give us some clues," Prue suggested.

"*Book of Shadows,* here we come!" Phoebe declared.

Prue gathered up the now-dry photographs, and the three Halliwells headed up to the attic.

Piper had barely touched the thick book when the covers burst open, straight to the page of symbols. "That was a time-saver," she commented. She raised her eyes heavenward. "Thanks."

"Okay, let's figure this out." Prue laid the photographs beside the illustrations in the book. She ran her finger along the page. She peered carefully at something, then raised her eyes to her sisters. "The carvings on the bow are a spell for power over animals."

"Wow," Phoebe commented. "So Ivan's act is really thanks to this violin, not anything special that he's doing. Well, that's kind of disappointing."

"It also means that he could have used the violin to make the animals attack us," Piper added.

"Maybe . . ." Prue murmured. She went back to studying the images. "Actually, the painted symbols on the back of the violin modify the spell on the bow, and build in protections and warnings."

"What do you mean?" Phoebe asked.

"The power over animals is based on the nature of the player," Prue explained. She looked up at her sisters again. "That makes sense. The animals are responding to the sweet and gentle Ivan that I've encountered."

"And the animals attacked because they were responding to the nasty Ivan I've met?" Phoebe asked. "Maybe."

"But he didn't have the violin with him when those animals got out," Prue said.

"Adding to the theory that there are two of him," Piper said.

"I don't know how anyone else could have gotten hold of the violin," Prue said. "I watched Ivan lock it in the company safe. He's extra careful with it now."

Now Piper studied the book. "This is something. It says here that the power can follow the violin only if the instrument is freely given. Otherwise the violin will always return to its owner."

"That explains its rematerialization," Prue said excitedly. "Someone must have stolen it, and the violin returned to Ivan. He was afraid it had been taken. In fact, he had been out looking for it when it reappeared in front of me."

"Does *The Book of Shadows* say anything else?" Phoebe asked.

Piper scanned the page. She nodded. "If the owner dies, the violin and its powers go to whatever family member touches it first."

"Let me see that," Phoebe asked, moving closer to the heavy book.

"I think we have an idea of what's going on," Piper suggested as she stepped aside to make room for Phoebe. "There really is an Ivan twin. He must be some kind of relative, and he wants that violin."

"Is there more about Gypsy magic in here?" Phoebe asked, riffling through the pages. "Oh, here's something."

"What?" Prue asked.

"Some Gypsy beliefs," Phoebe said. "It almost reads like my textbook from the folklore class I took. Mostly the stuff Ivan told you about: the love spells, the Romany ruby."

"The threefold power gem," Piper remembered. "Olga mentioned it, too. It must be big in Gypsy magical systems."

"This is all very interesting," Prue commented. "But I'm more concerned with why someone would go to such lengths for this violin. Why would anyone care so much about getting tigers to dance?"

"I think I know why." Phoebe tapped the page she was consulting. Piper leaned in close to peer at the picture painted on it.

A horrifying monster glared back at her from *The Book of Shadows*. The beast had the powerful front body of a lion, but its back half looked like a gigantic lizard. It had twelve eyes that burned with evil and a double set of enormous teeth. A spiky row of tusks circled its neck and its face was uglier than any dragon Piper had ever imagined. The word "Loriathian" was written underneath the illustration. She quickly read the text accompanying the drawing.

Piper took in a deep breath, then looked up at Prue. "It's not tigers someone wants to use the violin to control. It's the Loriathian."

CHAPTER
16

Prue stared at the picture of the Loriathian. It was a horrible-looking creature.

"What is that thing, and why does someone want to control it?" Prue said.

"Look at it," Phoebe said. "Between you and it, who would you prefer to be in charge?"

"Got a point," Prue replied. "But really, Piper, what's its story?"

Piper started to read from the book. "Let's see. 'The Loriathian guards the Romany ruby on the astral plane. The only way to get the gem is by distracting, killing, or otherwise defeating the Loriathian. So far, no Gypsy has been able to do so in over five hundred years.' "

Prue put it together. "So whoever is after Ivan's violin plans to use it to placate or soothe the Loriathian long enough to snatch the gem."

"That would be my guess," Phoebe said.

"And that's where all the rumors about Ivan started—the bad luck is the result of someone trying to steal the violin."

"Or scare him into giving it over." Prue began pacing as the elements all clicked into place. "Ivan said that Olga had tried to convince him that the violin was cursed and that she would be willing to take it off his hands."

"That way the violin's power would transfer from Ivan to her, since he'd be giving it to her freely," Piper said slowly, picking up Prue's train of thought.

"Olga. She's also a Gypsy. She knows all about the Romany ruby," Phoebe said. "She must be behind this."

"She's also the one who sent us to find Prue, and instead we found a pack of hungry animals," Piper added. "You know, I thought she might have guessed that we were Charmed Ones. So she used some kind of charm that protected the animals from our power. They were just doing what wild animals do—go wild."

"But she can't be doing this alone," Prue said. "She isn't any kind of ringer for Ivan."

"Could she be a shape-shifter?" Piper asked.

Prue thought for a moment. "I don't think so. I saw her hanging around the ring when Phoebe was being grilled by Ivan number two in the trailer."

"So we're back to figuring out who her accomplice is," Phoebe said. "At least we know what they want."

"I think we know one of her accomplices," Piper said. "The Gypsy zombie." She explained to Prue what she and Phoebe had discovered about the ghoulish creature Prue had encountered that first day, and about their own battle with it earlier. "Powerful Gypsies use them to do their dirty work."

"They're up to some pretty dirty work, too," Prue said quietly. "They've tried stealing, coercion, and attempted murder."

"The fire," Phoebe said. "They hoped Ivan would be inside. They knew the violin would survive."

"Instead, they killed Miranda," Prue said. Her eyes widened with alarm. "We have to warn Ivan." She smacked her forehead. "Oh, no! We just left him there. I tossed him into the bushes and we left him there with the animals."

"I have a feeling Ivan had no trouble handling the animals," Phoebe assured her. "It's the time-freezing and telekinesis angle that may need explaining."

"Actually, his witnessing our powers may have been a good thing," Prue commented. "Ivan doesn't believe in magic. Now he's going to have to. It may help when we explain to him what is going on."

"And that he's in danger," Piper added. "Maybe now he'll believe that."

"Okay, but who is he in danger from, aside from Olga?"

"How could we not have noticed a dude with Ivan's face?" Phoebe said. "He has a very memorable face."

"We're not the only ones who didn't notice," Piper pointed out. "If Ivan had a dead ringer at the circus, everyone would have said something."

Prue remembered all the circus habits Kristin had prattled on about over the last few days. There was something in all that trivia. . . .

The answer hit Prue like a lightning bolt. "Not if the twin is known by another face—a clown face."

"We have to go back to the carnival," Phoebe said. "We have to warn Ivan, and we have to find out who is behind this so we can stop them."

Piper nodded. "These aren't the kind of Gypsies I want with threefold power."

"You're forgetting something," Piper pointed out. "Olga knows about us. She and her accomplice will be on the lookout."

"You're right. And we already know how far they're willing to go." Prue bit her lip, thinking. "So how can we do this safely?"

Phoebe's eyes lit up with an idea. "I know exactly how we can poke around the circus," she declared.

She slung an arm over Prue's shoulder. "Only you're not going to like it, sister dear."

Prue tugged at her bright orange fright wig, trying to keep it on her head. She was wearing white makeup with a bright red nose and a large mustache. All three Halliwells were sporting facial hair. They also wore very baggy clothes, trying to look as boyish as possible. They had remembered that Masha was the only female clown in the company. Good thing they did— they didn't want to blow their cover immediately.

"I am not a happy camper," Prue grumbled. Not only was she wearing a ridiculous getup, she and her sisters had arrived at the carnival at the crack of dawn. Make that *before* the crack of dawn, she thought, gazing at the dark sky. A tiny little pink glow appeared just at the horizon line through the trees in Golden Gate Park.

"We want to try to catch the clowns without their makeup on," Piper reminded Prue. "We have a chance only if we catch them just as they're waking up."

"Oh, goody," Prue said. "So we get to play clown Peeping Toms."

"At least they won't know it's us spying on them," Phoebe said.

"Actually, I think I'm more worried about what *I* might see, than I am about them seeing me," Piper said.

They parked the car far from the parking lot so that they wouldn't draw any attention to themselves. As they crept along the outskirts of the trailers that formed Clown Alley, Prue stopped her sisters. "Wait," she whispered. She yanked her sisters into the bushes.

A figure slipped through the trees ahead of them. He was wearing Ivan's trademark tight black pants and boots.

He must have heard a branch crack or somehow become aware of their presence. He turned—and Prue found herself gazing at Ivan's face.

Luckily, he didn't seem to spot the Halliwells.

"Which one is he?" Phoebe whispered.

"I'll find out," Prue said. "You follow him to see what trailer he goes into. No matter what, don't lose him."

"Got it." Phoebe nodded. She and Piper sneaked out of the bushes as quickly and as quietly as they could.

Prue shut her eyes. She concentrated really hard, picturing herself in Ivan's temporary quarters since losing his trailer in the fire. Mr. Amalfi had given Ivan permission to sleep in an equipment trailer on the other side of the carnival.

Gathering her energy, she astral projected out of her body. A moment later she gazed down at Ivan's sleeping form. He lay on a mattress on the floor, surrounded by electrical equipment.

There *are* two of them! Prue thought with glee. I was right—this Ivan is a sweet and hunky human. Not an evil bone in his body.

And what a body.

She couldn't help herself. She reached out and pulled the blanket back up over his bare chest. He must have kicked the covers off in his sleep. He murmured and rolled over onto his side.

"Better get out of here before I get into trouble," she told herself.

Again she concentrated and brought herself back into her body. She felt a little woozy. She wasn't sure if she'd ever get used to her ability to astral project. She loved it, but it was really disconcerting to travel in and out of her body. Even more so, since that body was currently dressed in a clown outfit.

Piper and Phoebe were nowhere in sight. Prue figured they were still tracking the Ivan look-alike. She crept out of the bushes and scurried along the trailers of Clown Alley, trying to figure out where her sisters had gone.

A door on a trailer popped open. A tall, bald man with a large, pointy nose stepped out and stretched. A moment later a plump woman with short black hair followed him.

That must be Kaboodle and Masha's trailer, Prue realized.

Uh-oh. Busted. "Hello, there," Kaboodle said. "You're up early."

Prue didn't want her voice to give her away as a girl, so she just waved and nodded. She picked up her pace to pass his trailer as quickly as possible.

Kaboodle looked at Prue carefully. "That's a new costume," he commented. "Working up a new character?"

Prue nodded.

His eyebrows knit together. "You should really run this by the directors and me before changing an act."

Prue held up her hands and waved them back and forth, indicating he had the wrong idea.

"Oh, he probably just wants to get it right before he shows it to you," Masha said, coming to Prue's defense.

Prue put one finger on her nose and pointed the other at Masha and nodded.

"You see?" Masha said. "Stop being such a dictator."

Prue was very grateful that neither Masha nor Kaboodle found it strange that she was communicating in mime. One side benefit of the weirdness of clowns, she figured.

"The quality of the act is very important to me," Kaboodle protested.

Masha sniffed. "Being important is what's important to you," she said. "We all know you're in charge. Give the boy his creative freedom." She turned and stepped back into the trailer.

"That's unfair," Kaboodle complained. He followed his wife inside and slammed the door.

Prue felt badly that she had caused a fight between the couple, but she didn't have time to think about it just then. She and her sisters had some evil Gypsies to stop—before it was too late.

What would the threefold power of the Romany ruby do for them? she wondered. Was this part of some kind of Gypsy power struggle? Ivan had mentioned that there were sometimes warring factions among the Gypsy families. Was grabbing the ruby a grab for control over all the families?

Even if it was, would it stop there? Did they have larger, more universal plans? Obviously these people were ruthless.

With that discomforting thought in mind, Prue picked up her pace. Only she wasn't sure where to look.

Luckily she didn't have to wonder—or wander—for long. Two clowns with familiar outfits were heading toward her.

"Ivan was asleep!" Prue burst out.

"Well, someone's awfully tickled about Ivan's innocence," Piper noted.

"Didn't I tell you he wasn't evil?" Prue said.

"I think Prue's just really pleased to be right," Phoebe teased. "She just hates it when she's wrong."

"And when would that be?" Prue said with a wicked grin.

"Stop before we hit you with a pie in the face," Piper quipped.

"At least we're appropriately dressed," Phoebe said. "Okay, enough about how wonderful it is that your guy isn't the one we're after."

"We know who it is, now," Piper said. "That new clown, Sacha. We followed him straight to his trailer."

"And guess who showed up just as the sun began to rise," Phoebe added.

Prue crossed her arms over her chest. "Olga." It wasn't a question, just a statement.

"Affirmative," Phoebe said. "They are definitely in cahoots."

"Relatives, actually. Ivan, I mean, Sacha," Piper corrected herself, "called her Mama Olga."

"Pretty freaky that two different women could give birth to identical twins," Prue commented.

"Since we became witches, I'd say we excelled in all things freaky," Phoebe said. "We can worry about the hows of all this later. Now let's figure out the whats."

"As in *what* do we do now," Prue agreed.

"And the answer is . . . ?" Piper asked.

Frustrated, Prue raked her hand through her hair, until she realized she was tugging on orange yarn. "I think we should tell Ivan everything. He may know some Gypsy lore about this that may help."

"As you said," Phoebe pointed out, "he's got to believe in magic now."

"Besides, there's bound to be another attempt on Ivan's life," Prue said. "Nothing else they've done has worked—not the zombies, not the thefts."

Piper shuddered. "They aren't the types to take no for an answer."

"So let's get over to Ivan's," Prue said. She glanced down at herself. "I just wish he didn't have to see me like this."

"As long as we're here, we keep these disguises," Phoebe ordered. "Remember, Olga and Sacha are probably after us, too."

"I know. You're right." Prue struck a pose. "Do I look sexy like this?"

Piper and Phoebe glanced at each other. "No," they said in unison.

"You might qualify as cute, maybe, if you're into Raggedy Ann or Andy," Piper said.

Prue led the way to Ivan's trailer on the other side of the lot. The sun had completely risen. She hadn't realized how early the carnival kicked into gear. Many employees were already heading for the food trailer, and the crew were already at the tent, checking the rigging.

"Wow. I just changed my mind about wanting to run off with the circus," Phoebe commented. "These people get up way too early to suit me."

As the sisters crossed the midway, booth operators were setting up all around them. Everyone ignored them. Prue was pleased at how well the disguises were working.

"Glad to see you're early for the brush-up rehearsal," a voice called out as they passed the tent.

"Is he talking to us?" Piper whispered to her sisters.

"Keep going, and keep your head down," Prue ordered.

Several clowns appeared in front of them carrying props. "Hi," one of them said. "If you're looking for breakfast, no such luck."

"Kaboodle fixed it so that the cook wouldn't serve clowns during the rehearsal," the short one complained. He tossed several juggling balls into the air.

"Give up on sneaking away," the first one said in a low voice. "Kaboodle is two feet behind you. Man, he's such a dictator."

By now all five of the clowns in front of them were juggling different objects. Whispering a silent apology, Prue used her telekinesis to send all the props flying.

"Run!" she cried. She banged right into a clown riding on a unicycle. He crashed into Kaboodle.

"That should keep them busy for a few minutes," she panted as she ran alongside her sisters.

"It will be tough to explain how it happened," Phoebe commented.

"By the time they get inside the tent, they'll have worked it into their new act," Prue assured her.

They made it all the way to Ivan's temporary quarters without another incident. Being a clown really did make a person anonymous, Prue noted.

Prue knocked on the trailer door. "Come in," came a groggy voice.

Prue, Phoebe, and Piper stepped inside. The trailer was packed with lighting equipment, cables, and tools. Ivan was sitting up, in a pair of jeans and a T-shirt. His eyebrows rose at the sight of his visitors.

"Can I help you?" he asked.

"Ivan, it's me," Prue said. "Prue."

Ivan's big brown eyes traveled up and down her body. She really wished she hadn't had to hide the fact she was a woman when she'd created her disguise. She could have at least come up with a sexy clown costume.

Ivan burst out laughing. "Have you all become

infected with the circus virus? We always get a few in every town we play."

"No, it's nothing like that," Prue said. "This is actually serious." She glanced down at herself. "In spite of our appearances."

Prue explained everything they knew: about the Romany ruby. About the zombie. The attempts on Ivan's violin and on his life. And about the magic of his violin.

That was the hardest part to tell. Harder than the fact that there were people out to kill him. Or that Prue and her sisters were witches. Throughout all the lengthy, disturbing story, filled with upsetting revelations and her sisters' interruptions, Ivan's face remained open and understanding.

But now his brown eyes darkened. He gazed deep into Prue's. "Do you mean it is all the magic of the violin?" he asked softly. Prue's heart ached to see the pain and embarrassment on his face. "I—I am nothing?"

She took his hand in hers. "Don't say that. You play beautifully."

Ivan stood and turned away from them. "Perhaps I don't play at all. Perhaps it is all the violin. And my skill with the animals—it is simply some kind of trick."

"Nothing about magic is simple," Phoebe said. "Believe us—we've found out the hard way."

"And I've seen you with the animals when you're not playing. You have a gift with them," Prue assured him.

Ivan ducked his head, his shoulders slumped. "It could still be a magic spell. You have said you don't really know how the violin works."

"Look, I know you feel bad and everything," Phoebe cut in. "But we've got a big problem to solve fast."

Ivan took a deep breath and turned back to face them. "You know, I never believed in the old stories or in the superstitions. But I know what I saw with my own eyes last night." He rubbed his backside. "And what I felt when I landed in those bushes."

"Sorry about that," Prue said.

He smiled at her sadly. "You did the right thing. You were protecting your sisters. You had no reason to think I wasn't the terrible man in the vision."

"Well, if it makes you feel any better," Phoebe piped up, "Prue was always on your side. Except for maybe that one minute in the woods."

Ivan took Prue's hand in both of his. "Thank you," he said.

Prue wished with all her heart that she could take away the pain that she knew this knowledge caused him. She hated that she was the one to have shattered the belief he had in his own talent. He had so much startling information to deal with and no time in which to process any of it. Even his heritage was now in question. His parents denied the legends, yet he was caught up right in the middle of one of the most dangerous.

Ivan nodded with resolve and turned from Prue to face Phoebe. "You're right," he said, strength and conviction returning to his deep voice. "We have a big problem to solve."

"Can you think of anything from the legends that might help us?" Piper asked. "About the Loriathian or the Romany ruby?"

"Or why you would have a twin?" Phoebe added.

Ivan leaned against a tall metal shelving unit and shook his head.

"What exactly is your relationship to Olga?" Prue asked.

"None that I know of, but we do speak a similar dialect. She may be a distant cousin or something."

"Think, Ivan," Prue pressed. "We really need some clues."

His face clouded. "You know, there is a superstition among Gypsies that twin boys must be raised apart."

"That could explain it," Phoebe said. "Right there."

Confusion played across Ivan's features. "But I can't imagine my parents following the old ways."

"Maybe having to give away a baby boy is what turned them against the superstitions and legends," Prue suggested gently. "It would certainly make me question my family's traditions."

Ivan nodded slowly. "You may be right. And it may explain how Olga knew about the violin in the first place."

"So what do we do now?" Prue looked at her sisters and then back at Ivan.

What she saw made her gasp.

Ivan was shimmering. The outlines of his body were growing indistinct. Swirls of energy danced around him.

"Ivan!" she cried.

A roaring sound filled the room, as if a great tearing in the fabric of the universe were taking place. A wind whipped up, sending objects flying around the trailer.

"What's happening?" Piper shrieked as she ducked a light stand.

"I don't know!" Prue shouted back.

"Ivan's breaking up!" Phoebe screamed.

"If he's going somewhere," Prue cried, "so am I!"

Prue concentrated, astral projected herself into the energy swirling around Ivan, and gripped his arm.

One moment later she and Ivan were adrift in what Prue could only imagine was the astral plane.

Home of the Loriathian.

CHAPTER
17

Eerie lights pulsed all around Prue. She felt as if she was floating, but she wasn't moving. Everything shimmered. In fact, if she weren't so frightened, the sight would be quite beautiful—as if she were living inside starlight. There didn't seem to be any up, down, left, or right. No landscape.

Nothing but Ivan, Sacha, and Olga.

And the Loriathian.

The enormous and hideous creature lay just in front of a glowing area. Its twelve eyes each burned a different color, none of them pretty. Its razor-sharp teeth hung over its lips, and its forked tongue darted in and out. It was aware of their presence, and on alert, but was clearly waiting and watching to see what they would do.

"What are you doing here?" Olga screamed at Prue and Ivan. Only her mouth never moved. On the astral plane, Prue guessed, they were all telepathic.

"We're going to stop you," Prue thought back.

Olga laughed a nasty, evil laugh. It sent strange waves rippling through the astral plane. Prue realized if she was going to use any of her powers in the astral plane, she'd better start adjusting, fast.

She moved an arm, just to test the waters. Glowing energy particles parted around her limb.

"Why?" Ivan pleaded. "Just tell me that." He looked over at Sacha. "And who are you? Why do we look the same?"

"Meet your brother, Ivan," Olga said.

Ivan floated backward, as if he'd been hit by her words. Prue reached out and laid a hand on his shoulder. He reached up and clutched it.

She sent a sense of strength and resolve into the hand Ivan held, hoping it would help him. Her hand grew warmer in his, and in a few moments she could feel his grip become less panicked and much more powerful.

"I suppose it would be good for you to know the truth," Olga said to Ivan. "You may be of use."

Her long hair floated around her head, weightless in the astral plane. As she tossed her head, shimmering waves rippled away from her. Prue studied every move the woman made, trying to understand the energy surrounding them all.

"As is our family's way," Olga explained to Ivan, "you twin boys were separated at birth. Sacha came to live with me, a distant relative. It broke your foolish mother's heart."

Olga's face twisted into an ugly, patronizing sneer. Prue felt Ivan stiffen in anger. She sent more thoughts his way. Stay calm. Don't let her get to you.

"What broke *my* heart was that Sacha had been cheated out of his inheritance," Olga continued, her voice rising. "They wasted that violin on you. You never even understood its power. Your family turned their backs on the dark arts, but not mine. Your family wasted their gifts, becoming silly performers. We worked for generations perfecting our magical skills. We deserve that violin. It is wasted in your clumsy hands."

Prue checked the Loriathian again. It still hadn't moved, but she could sense its unleashed power. It was biding its time, and Prue knew that was what she must do, too.

She glanced at Sacha. He had remained silent, obviously completely under Olga's thumb. She wondered if Olga had ever actually cared for him or only for his access to the violin.

Olga's expression changed. A sly, calculating look appeared in her eyes. "Until now," she crooned. "Now you have a chance to finally use the violin for its intended purpose—to increase power. You will play that violin and lull the Loriathian, allowing me to take possession of the Romany ruby."

"Forget it," Ivan snapped.

"I want that ruby!" Olga shouted. "I refuse to continue to be the poor relation. Once I have my power manifested threefold all of the families will look up to me. And then watch me. I will be unstoppable!"

"I won't do it," Ivan declared. "I will not help you."

He held the violin out to Sacha. "Take it. I give it freely. I want no part of this. You can have the ruby for all I care."

"No," Prue protested, shocked by Ivan's action. "Don't you see? They shouldn't have the ruby. They're dangerous."

"Shut up," Olga snarled. "He is doing the right thing. Besides, he cannot fight us. Sacha is Ivan's nearest relative. All I need to do is kill Ivan and the violin becomes ours."

"Thanks, brother," Sacha said, snatching the violin and bow from Ivan. His voice had none of Ivan's warmth.

"Go, my son," Olga instructed. "Go and get what's mine."

Sacha nodded. He lifted the bow and approached the Loriathian. He began to play.

Rage filled Prue. Every note seemed to send another violent thought through her.

Sacha didn't play badly; the notes were clear and true. But they triggered horrifying images, and Prue's whole body shuddered with the evil darkness of the song.

The Loriathian opened its huge mouth and roared. Its tusks burst into position, forming a deadly collar around its massive neck, and it unsheathed its lionlike claws. The Loriathian bellowed in agony, the sound sending shards of energy swirling throughout the astral plane. Its dragon head twitched rhythmically, twitched in time with the song's meter, Prue noted.

That's it! Prue's heart pounded with this new knowledge. They don't understand, Prue realized. The violin reflects the player's soul. Sacha has a dark and evil soul. The music won't soothe the beast—it will stir it up.

The Loriathian lifted its heavy front paw, its claws dripping venom. Ivan was standing right within its reach!

Prue concentrated and sent Ivan hurtling away from the beast. She noticed that on the astral plane, her magical powers manifested themselves as glittering balls of energy, and those glowing orbs pushed Ivan out of range. Once the fireballs accomplished their task, they dissipated into swirling sparks.

The Loriathian roared again. Sacha played more furiously, obviously thinking the violin's power would kick in. Instead, Ivan's evil twin was infuriating the beast. Convulsive ripples shuddered through the reptile portion of the Loriathian's repulsive body, as if Sacha's playing was making it physically ill. It lifted a gigantic paw again to take a swipe at Sacha.

"No!" Olga shrieked. Then she began to chant quickly in a language Prue didn't understand. Frantically Olga pulled herbs from a charm bag she wore around her neck and flung them toward the Loriathian. Fireballs formed in front of her, just like the ones Prue's magic had created. Olga's chant grew stronger, and she hurled the fireballs at the Loriathian, knocking its paw away from Sacha. He continued to play the violin.

So Olga can also move objects, Prue observed, but her telekinetic ability is different. She has to resort to chants and herbs. Her way takes longer, Prue realized. I have the advantage.

The Loriathian thrashed and moaned, desperate to stop the despicable, torturous music.

I know how it feels, Prue thought. She hated the sick, evil feeling that was growing inside her.

"Why isn't it working?" Olga shrieked.

In outraged agony, the Loriathian stretched its long dragonlike snout forward, directly over Sacha.

"No!" Olga screamed again.

Still, Sacha kept playing. Prue's body was rigid with the monstrous anger the music created in her.

Olga chanted again, sending more fireballs to stop the Loriathian from attacking Sacha. Prue channeled the terrible energy of the music and used it to deflect every bit of Olga's magic.

The fireballs crackled and burst into a spray of sparks as they missed their target. In one ghastly move, the Loriathian swooped down and snatched Sacha up in its gaping, yawning mouth. In two bites, the beast swallowed him whole. Then it spit out the violin as though the instrument had burned its tongue.

"You!" Olga screamed at Prue. The fortune-teller flung herself toward Prue with the power of insane fury.

"Not a chance!" Prue shouted. Violent urges filled Prue's very essence. Part of her brain knew they were the result of magic, knew that once the music left her she'd be fine. But right now she let loose every ounce of bile and hostility in Olga's direction.

Right into the path of the Loriathian.

The rampaging beast snatched the woman up and tossed her above its head. Her terrified wails were cut off suddenly when it sank its teeth deep into her. It swallowed her, too.

The Loriathian let out a bellowing roar. The terrible music had infected it completely, taking it over.

Its twelve eyes burned with evil fire. The forked tongue flicked toward Prue, who sensed that she'd be its next victim.

"Prue!" Ivan called. "The violin!"

Prue concentrated hard and used her power to pull the instrument away from the creature. Then she sent it through astral space to Ivan.

The Loriathian's tail thrashed impatiently. It seemed to be preparing to pounce on Prue.

A clear, pure note sent glorious ripples through the astral plane. All twelve eyes of the Loriathian stared at Ivan.

Ivan began to play, the music pulling him closer to Prue. The melody soared and dipped, each variation gently soothing. Prue felt the anger leaving her body in waves.

Gradually, the Loriathian settled down, wrapping its reptilian tail around itself and curling into a ball. It was soon sleeping, its massive sides rising and falling with its deep breaths.

Just beyond the sleeping beast was a spinning gem. It hovered in space, slowly turning. It glowed with inner fire, a deep and rich red.

"The Romany ruby," Prue murmured.

Ivan and Prue floated in the astral plane, staring at the ruby, allowing themselves to return to a more peaceful state.

"It's beautiful," Prue finally said. She glanced at Ivan. "Aren't you going to take it?"

Ivan shook his head. "I don't want power. All I've ever wanted was my music and my animals. That's all I need for the kind of power I want."

Prue smiled, unsurprised by his answer.

Ivan sighed a deep and thoughtful sigh. "And now it is over," he declared.

"Not quite," Prue said. "The next question is, how do we get back to our world? It was Olga's magic that brought us here."

CHAPTER
18

Ivan gaped at Prue. "You—you don't know how to get us back?" he stammered.

"Don't panic," Prue said, trying not to panic herself. "I think if I grab onto you and astral project back into my body, we'll return to our world. I just hope we don't end up switching bodies or something."

"That could happen?" Ivan asked.

"No, of course not," Prue lied. She'd seen all sorts of things happen, but she didn't want to worry Ivan. He was worried enough.

"Okay, put your arms around me," she instructed Ivan.

"Gladly," Ivan said. He embraced her closely.

Even in her astral form, it felt good to be held by him. Prue nestled against his chest and shut her eyes.

"Wait a sec." Prue pulled herself a few inches away from Ivan. "Too distracting the other way," she explained. "I have to concentrate."

Prue felt the familiar surge of energy as her astral form found its way back to her true world body. Keeping her eyes shut, she patted herself up and down. Yup. There's that goofy clown outfit. She opened her eyes. And there's Ivan's handsome face, smiling at me, as he holds up his violin. They were in the equipment trailer, where they had been before their little detour into astral space.

"Well, it's about time!" Phoebe snapped. "Things have been all crazy here." She gestured out the window.

Prue glanced outside. "Uh-oh." Ivan's animals were frozen in attack positions. Some people were frozen with their hands around each other's throats, about to deck each other. Others were obviously in screaming matches. "What is going on here?"

"We don't know. All of a sudden everyone went loco. Mean. The animals went berserk first, and then, well, as you can see, everyone seriously got on everyone else's nerves.

The music, Prue realized. It broke through from the astral plane. It sent violent thoughts through me, too.

"Are you two all right?" Prue asked her sisters.

Piper and Phoebe looked sheepish. "Well, we were kind of snappy with each other," Phoebe admitted, "but we had some stuff to concentrate on."

"Like freezing an entire circus," Piper complained. "Do you have any idea if they'll go back to normal once they unfreeze. Or are they still going to be fighting?"

"I know what to do." Ivan placed the violin under his chin and led the Halliwells out of the trailer. The moment they stepped outside he began to play.

As Ivan's music filled the air, Prue was once again filled with a calm, peaceful feeling. She took each of her sisters' hands, and they watched the chaotic scene unfreeze. The animals went back to peaceful poses. The fighting crew members looked startled and apologized to one another. All around her, Prue heard, "I don't know what came over me." And "Don't know what got into me" and "No hard feelings, right?" Within minutes the circus resumed normal activity.

Prue turned to Ivan. "It isn't the power of the violin alone," she said. "Sacha had the instrument, and in his hands it was an instrument of destruction. In your hands there is an entirely different effect."

Ivan smiled. "I have always loved the music of my family. I love to play, and I love to see how my beautiful animals respond."

"That's it," Prue realized. "You put your heart into your playing. That's the real magic."

"I need to get ready for my performance," Ivan apologized. "Thank you. For everything." He held the violin up high and then wrapped Prue in a warm embrace. Then he kissed her cheek and took off.

All three Halliwells let out long, dreamy sighs as he strode away.

"Omigod!" a shrill voice called out behind her. Prue turned around and saw an astonished Kristin jogging toward her. "You three look soooooo adorable," Kristin gushed.

Prue glanced down. Oh, right. The costume.

"I am so pleased that you decided to join the Caring Clowns," Kristin bubbled. "That will make a great ending to the article. Jaded photographer won· over by the circus."

Prue shook her head but didn't bother to correct Kristin. Of course, she'd have to explain later that this was her first and last appearance as a clown. But for now, she wanted to bask in the warm feeling left by Ivan's music.

"We'd better go change," Piper said.

"Yeah, or else Kaboodle will make us rehearse."

"And I need to hand out my thank-you notes," Kristin said. "I like the personal touch." She waved a batch of small envelopes at Prue. Each had a little pink smiley face drawn on it. "See you later," Kristin called over her shoulder as she marched toward the circus tent.

Phoebe draped her arm over Prue's shoulders. "You know, Kristin had a good idea. The clowns have one open spot."

"Yeah," Piper added, sidling up on Prue's other side. "Sacha won't be back for the show. Maybe you'd like to step in for him. You already have a costume."

Prue smirked at her sisters. "Hah. Not a chance."

"Well, I still think I want to volunteer for the Caring Clowns," Piper said, pulling off her mustache.

"Me, too," Phoebe seconded. "How about it, Prue?"

Prue shook her head. "No way. The one thing this experience has confirmed is what I knew all along."

"What's that?" asked Piper.

Prue grinned. "Stay away from clowns!"

About the Author

CARLA JABLONSKI is an actress, director, and writer living in New York City. She is the author of several books in the Adventures of Wishbone series: *Homer Sweet Homer* (inspired by *The Odyssey*), *The Legend of Sleepy Hollow*, *20,000 Wags Under the Sea* (based on Jules Verne's classic), *The Scent of the Vampire* (an adaptation of Dracula), and Tales of Terror (an anthology of scary stories). For Pocket Books she has written *Clueless: Southern Fried Makeover*. She has edited books for The Hardy Boys Mystery Stories and R. L. Stine's Give Yourself Goosebumps, and co-created the new interactive mystery series, Digital Detectives. Carla Jablonski spent summer 2000 working for the Big Apple Circus in upstate New York, helping the directors ready the show for the new season. She is training on the trapeze for a play she will be doing in spring 2001.

"I'm the Idea Girl, the one who can always think of something to do."

VIOLET EYES

A spellbinding new novel of the future

by Nicole Luiken

Angel Eastland knows she's different. It's not just her violet eyes that set her apart. She's smarter than her classmates and more athletically gifted. Her only real competition is Michael Vallant, who also has violet eyes—eyes that tell her they're connected, in a way she can't figure out.

Michael understands Angel. He knows her dreams, her nightmares, and her most secret fears. Together they begin to realize that nothing around them is what it seems. Someone is watching them, night and day. They have just one desperate chance to escape, one chance to find their true destiny, but their enemies are powerful—and will do anything to stop them.

3074

"YOU'RE DEAD. YOU DON'T BELONG HERE."

SUSANNAH JUST TRAVELED A GAZILLION MILES FROM NEW YORK TO CALIFORNIA IN ORDER TO LIVE WITH A BUNCH OF STUPID BOYS (HER NEW STEPBROTHERS). SHE HASN'T EVEN UNPACKED YET, SHE'S MADE HER MOTHER PRACTICALLY CRY ALREADY, AND NOW THERE'S A GHOST SITTING IN HER NEW BEDROOM. TRUE, JESSE'S A VERY ATTRACTIVE GUY GHOST, BUT THAT'S NOT THE POINT.

LIFE HASN'T BEEN EASY THESE PAST SIXTEEN YEARS. THAT'S BECAUSE SUSANNAH'S A MEDIATOR—A CONTACT PERSON FOR JUST ABOUT ANYBODY WHO CROAKS, LEAVING THINGS...WELL, UNTIDY. AT LEAST JESSE'S NOT DANGEROUS. UNLIKE HEATHER, THE ANGRY GIRL GHOST HANGING OUT AT SUSANNAH'S NEW HIGH SCHOOL....

READ *SHADOWLAND*

BOOK #1 OF
THE MEDIATOR
BY JENNY CARROLL

3043-01